WHITE LUNG

Other books by Grant Buday

Monday Night Man

The Venetian

Under Glass

White Lung

A NOVEL BY
Grant Buday

ANVIL PRESS PUBLISHERS

Printed and bound in Canada
First Edition
Cover Design: Derrick Carter

Canadian Cataloguing in Publication Data

Buday, Grant, 1956-
White lung

ISBN 1-895636-20-5

I. Title
PS8553.U444W54 1999   C813'.54   C98-910394-3
PR9199.3.B7636W54 1999

Represented in Canada by the Literary Press Group
Distributed by General Distribution Services

The publisher gratefully acknowledges the assistance of the B.C. Arts Council and the Canada Council for the Arts.

Le Conseil des Arts | The Canada Council
du Canada | for the Arts

Anvil Press
Suite 204-A – 175 East Broadway,
Vancouver, BC V5T 1W2 CANADA

ACKNOWLEDGMENTS

Sections of *White Lung* were previously
published in *The Capilano Review, Event*
and *The Malahat Review.*

He laid his cheek against the soft of the bread, it was spongy and warm, alive. But he would very soon take that plush feel off it, by God but he would very quickly take that fat white look off its face.

<small>Samuel Beckett,</small> *More Pricks Than Kicks*

CHAPTER ONE

The Dough Deflates

KLAUS CARRIED THE GAS CAN low against his thigh, like an assassin concealing a pistol. He walked down the alley past the dumpsters and out to the sidewalk. He halted. Two blocks away a car idled at a light. The light went green and the car headed off. Klaus continued up the street and stopped at The Upper Crust. A sign in the window said: GOING OUT OF BUSINESS. He peered past it over top the frilled curtain. It was too dark to see. He'd been inside before, though. The floors were oak and the shelves pine. The Bavarian style oak door made him think of his father's shop. His main memory of his father was of him kneading dough, of him punching it, slamming it, beating it with his fists, hammering it with murderous fury. And yet the strange thing was how that dough always emerged in the form of sweet and elegant pastry.

Klaus studied the window for an alarm strip. There didn't seem to be one. He raised the gas can, punched in one of the panes, unscrewed the cap, and poured the gas through, checking the street as the furious smelling fuel splattered the floor inside. When the can was nearly empty he doused the oak door itself, stepped back, and discovered he'd forgotten the matches. He ran down to the corner, and as he turned slid in a puddle and landed on his hip. He sat there still holding the gas can. Then he limped up the alley to his Rabbit. The door was locked. Searching his coat and pants for the key he found nothing. He cupped his hands around his face and stared in the window. He was drunk but clear-headed. He reminded himself you couldn't lock your keys in a Rabbit because the lock required the key. Klaus was always patient and methodical when he'd been drinking. He retraced his steps to the corner, checking the ground all the way. The keys gleamed like a pile of dimes in the puddle. He got the matches, a box of REDBIRD Strike Anywhere Matches he kept in the glove box. When he made it back to the street he stopped. Two cars were sitting at the light. Cops. They were facing opposite directions, driver-door-to-driver-door, having a chat. He stepped behind a dumpster. The light changed but the cops stayed where they were. The light changed again. Klaus thought about the broken window. Was the gas evaporating? What if the cops went up the alley and saw his car? The ballast of beer in his belly steadied him. He was burning the shop because he was afraid to buy it. And there was no way it could just sit there and taunt him. So the shop had to go. Besides, he couldn't let Darlene discover it. Darlene was his wife. The fact that tomorrow was their twentieth wedding anniversary was something he refused to even think about. The cops began pulling away from each other. The tires of the car coming toward Klaus sucked the wet street. When the car had passed, Klaus limped to The Upper Crust. He lit a cluster of five matches and dropped it through the window. It died. He did it again. Then a third time. On the fourth try flames flowed across the floor like orange mildew.

§

Earlier that evening, Klaus went to a union meeting at the Cambrian Hall. Scotty Mutton was playing the fool, turning the meeting into a sideshow. He'd packed slices of white bread into wads as big and hard as lacrosse balls, then set up targets.

"Three balls for a buck!" Mutton pointed to the bottles arranged along the lip of the stage. The Welsh Men's Choir practised in the Cambrian Hall. Stale beers and half-finished rum and cokes were always left behind doors, on window ledges, and in the washroom. Mutton had found them all and set them up.

"Come on! Three for a buck!"

The bakers, however, ignored him, because they had other things on their minds. Seven days ago, a notice appeared in the coffee room detailing the company's demands—a 25% wage cut. Five twenty-five an hour. From $20.25 to $15. No discussion, no warning. The contract was up. It was take the cut or Vancouver Bestbuy closed.

"All right then," said Mutton. "Forget bottles. Bottles're for kids. Live targets. Anyone beans Keegan or Wong I'll give him twenty bucks." Keegan was union president, Wong the general manager, and they were due any minute. "Twenty dollars!" cried Mutton like a sideshow barker conning country rubes. Mutton was sixty-three, a jockey-sized Glaswegian with hair the colour of burlap. "Twenty for a knock on the nut." This offer caught more interest. Cracking Keegan or Wong on the head with a hardball of dough held distinct appeal.

"Is there a bonus for blood?"

Mutton smiled at Jeremy Bell with the fondness of

a master for a disciple. "Fuckin' right. Ten buck bonus for first blood."

Bell was a vegetarian and a Buddhist committed to nonviolence. He was wearing a yak wool coat made by Tibetan refugees. It had buttons of deodar. Bell was taking a course in religious studies at U.B.C. He'd informed Mutton that *deodar* meant 'wood of the gods' in Sanskrit. Mutton, who'd once been purcer on a freighter and spent many nights in Bombay's red-light district, informed Bell that *lingam* meant 'penis' in Sanskrit.

When Klaus had entered the hall that evening, Martin Epp was right behind him, talking fast.

"I seen the sign, Klaus. Goin' outa business. The Upper Crust. The one we been waitin' for." Epp's voice dropped in case anyone scooped them on their plan to quit Bestbuy and open their own bakery. "Perfect location, good equipment, shitloada customers."

Klaus chose the empty seat at the end of a row, so Epp had to sit in the one behind.

Epp sat forward, whispering so closely Klaus could smell the McDonald's coffee Epp had been drinking. "The Upper Crust, Klaus. Place is beggin' for us."

The nine cans of Beck's Klaus had drunk since getting off work that afternoon had reddened his cheeks. A fresh flat of twenty-four was waiting under the seat of his Rabbit. In his mind, twenty-four cans of beer offered more security than any collective agreement.

Epp said, "We can make our move."

Klaus didn't want to make a move. He wanted his earplugs. Wearing earplugs was like being in a private room with padded walls. No one could get him when he had his earplugs in. Klaus leaned forward, propping his head in his hands and plugging his ears with his thumbs. For eighteen months now he'd been oven man. He'd moved from graveyard shift janitor to morning shift oven-loader to get away from Epp.

"Finally get our asses outa here."

Klaus watched the others seat themselves. There were about forty bakers there. With the exception of Bell, most were middle-aged or older. Many had been at Bestbuy since the fifties. Klaus had been there twenty-one years, but it still surprised him how his co-workers dressed away from the plant. Some even had hobbies. Mutton, for instance, collected Nineteenth Century French pornography. It made Klaus realize they had lives separate from the bakery. That always caught him off guard.

Scotty Mutton continued working the crowd. "Twenty dollars to any man who'll bean Keegan or Wong. Twenty dollars. Or fifty for the both of them. Fifty-for-two."

The odd thing about Mutton, thought Klaus, was not his homosexuality, but that no one harassed him about it. Mutton had sailed in Canada's merchant marine until getting drummed out on bestiality charges.

As well as Bombay, he'd whored in Bangkok, Kuala Lumpur, Jakarta, and Sydney. Mutton was a well of sexual lore. He insisted there was a law on the books in Australia prohibiting a single male from riding in the back of a loaded sheep truck without supervision.

Klaus looked around at the other bakers. There was "Sourdough" Stahl, the day shift production foreman, off in a corner gnawing his fingernails. Everyone hated Stahl. There was Jeremy Bell with his magazine-ad profile, sipping a bottle of wheat grass juice.

Mutton sidled up to Bell and slipped a bread ball into the pocket of Bell's Tibetan coat.

Bell swam, skied, ran, and cycled. His thirty-two-speed road bike was pure titanium, handmade in Italy, and cost him six thousand dollars, five of which he still owed. His ski boots had cost him six hundred, his ski suit four, his goggles one-twenty. Part-time student and part-time baker, Bell was maxed-out on both his VISA and MasterCard, and overdrawn at the bank. A wage cut would kill his plans to kayak Belize next December.

Fingers lingering in the warmth of Bell's pocket, Mutton said, "I could blow a sweet tune on your flute, lad."

The doe-eyed Bell did his best to appear bored. He liked to keep the closet door shut at union meetings.

"Who else then?" said Mutton. "Who else wants everlasting fame and satisfaction?"

Epp slid his chair forward, bringing with it the bitterness of his coffee-tainted breath. "The Upper Crust, Klaus. It's beggin' us."

The Upper Crust. Klaus hoped Darlene hadn't heard it was for sale. Then he'd really be up against the wall. Ten years ago he and Darlene had made a plan: put in five more years, stockpile capital, then make the big move and start up on their own. But five years later he'd climbed the seniority ladder. What if the shop failed? He'd lose that seniority and be back at the bottom of the list. So he'd hesitated. Seniority meant security. Klaus had a degree in business administration, so had already been approached regarding the potential—in a few years—of a supervisorship. The lure of a supervisorship added another complication. And yet when Bestbuy finally came through and actually offered it, he turned it down. Darlene had asked whether that was such a good idea.

"I mean, you don't seem interested in going out on your own anymore."

Klaus heard her disappointment. "Go off half-cocked I'll end up like my old man."

Darlene tried to be patient. Klaus regularly raised the spectre of his father, who'd killed his marriage, his bakery, and ultimately himself through overwork and peppermint schnapps. Once again she repeated, "You're not your father, Klaus." Gripping a fistful of dirty-blonde hair, she picked at her split ends. Unlike Klaus, who'd ballooned to two-twenty on his diet of beer, Darlene, a coffee drinker, was lean. Working away at those split ends, she said, "Going out on your own was your idea. Remember? It's all you used to talk about. You had plans. But if you're content to load an oven the rest of your life, fine, go ahead, be my guest."

"In ten years I'll have my Silver 80."

Darlene had gagged. Klaus might as well have reserved them places in an old folks home. The Silver 80 was a pension equation: your age plus years of full-time employment. If they totalled 80, you could quit and receive eighty percent of your wage until you died. The Golden 90 was the next step. "In ten years you'll be fifty, Klaus!"

Klaus's reaction was to move downstairs into the cement-walled basement. For over a year now he'd been sleeping on an army cot by the furnace.

And then there was Epp. He and Klaus used to work graveyard together. In those days they'd meet at The Blue Boy before every shift and plan their own shop. Then a year-and-a-half ago Klaus left graveyard. He sacrificed the fifty-five cent an hour night shift bonus and took the six A.M. oven-loading job. He did it to escape Epp, who failed to see what everyone else saw, which was that Klaus was never going to quit Bestbuy and go out on his own.

Sitting in the Cambrian Hall, Klaus felt Epp's coffee breath on his neck. "Hell, Klaus, this place is dead. Five dollar cut. We're goin' backwards. We—"

"Here they are, lads. Laurel and Hardy!"

Klaus turned and saw Keegan and Wong walk in.

Hank Keegan, the union president and acting business rep, carried a ballot box under one arm and his briefcase under the other. C.P. Wong, the general manager of Vancouver Bestbuy, carried a bottle of codeines. Eight days ago they'd met at The Blue Boy pub, a vast hall lined with a beer-sodden carpet, where workers from the various riverside mills drank.

§

Keegan had arrived at The Blue Boy first. He'd been wearing a rust-brown sports coat that matched the colour of his teeth. His bifocals, low on his nose, gave him the air of a bookie. He sat at his usual table with his back to the wall. He knew Wong was coming from a meeting with some company wheel from Back East, and that the news would be bad.

When Wong finally showed, Keegan watched him swallow three codeine tablets as the waiter plunked down a couple of glasses. Keegan knew Wong was trying to be one of the boys by banging back that dog-pee draft the others put up with. Keegan reached for his pint of Guiness. A migraine sufferer himself, he granted Wong a minute for the pills to kick in. He tapped up a Players Plain, lit it with his silver Baker's Union lighter, and then sat back. Keegan was sixty, but looked seventy. He wheezed with flour-induced asthma, had gone through a double bypass the year before, had a son doing time in Matsqui for beating up a cop, and his wife was off on yet another bus trip to Reno. Always expecting the worst, he asked, "Well, how bad?"

Wong knew he wasn't referring to his headache. "It's free trade."

"Forty-five years in the bakeries I never seen nothing free yet."

"What they're prepared—"

Keegan stopped him. "*You.* It's not they, it's *you.*"

Wong exhaled patiently. He looked like a goldfish, short, chinless, glinting from his gold-framed glasses to his rings. "It's nothing to do with me, Hank. It's Back East."

"All you guys ever do is point the finger Back East."

"I don't make the decisions."

"That's right. They make themselves."

Wong got back to the point. "A roll-back."

Keegan's eyes went as hard and flat as frozen dimes.

"Five-and-a-quarter an hour," said Wong. "That or shut down." Done, he sat as far away as he could, out of Keegan's reach.

"A cut."

"That's right."

"In wages."

Wong nodded.

"Just like that."

"Or they shut down," repeated Wong.

"Let me get this straight. You're telling me in one week Vancouver Bestbuy could be closed?"

"It's the Seattle plant, Hank. Those guys work for nine dollars an hour. Even with the exchange—"

"I've seen the figures. Bestbuy's up eight percent this year."

"I know."

"You know?"

Wong shrugged. "I don't know." He turned his palms upward. "The big unions are finished."

"Well shit." Keegan could already see how the membership would take this. And the thing is, they'd blame him. His term was up in three months. They'd bounce him out. He'd be back on the floor slinging pans.

"It's not the fifties anymore, Hank. It's the nineties."

"You shut down Wilman's, you shut down Weston's, you shut down Empress. You put two hundred and eleven men out of work. Two hundred and eleven men with families and mortgages. Now you're at it again."

"Hey. If the bakery closes I'm out too."

"You any idea what they're gonna do to us when we step into that hall next week?" said Keegan.

§

Wong did. In the intervening time he ran through half his codeines. What he hadn't told Keegan was that the cut did not guarantee their jobs, it merely delayed the shutdown by about a year. But if they heard that they'd strike for sure, and Wong would get transferred to Seattle. Wong didn't want to go to Seattle.

Everyone in the Cambrian Hall watched Keegan and Wong take their places up front. The folding table was scarred with carved initials and sticky rings from slopped drinks. Keegan made a mental note to have a cloth laid down next time. That is, if there was a next time. Pulling his inhaler from his coat pocket he sprayed his throat, reached for his cigarettes, then forced himself to leave them. Since his bypass, he'd cut down from two packs a day to one, but there was nothing he could do about the flour dust he'd breathed since the age of fifteen. He looked out at the men who'd voted him into office. Forty years he'd known some of them. There was Scotty Mutton at the back next to young Jeremy Bell. There was John Sourdough Stahl. Keegan had worked with Stahl's father. There was Dan Donnelly. And there was Klaus Mann. Keegan admired

Klaus for turning down that supervisorship. He'd always hoped Klaus would get more active in the union, but all he seemed to be doing lately was getting more active with the bottle.

Jeremy Bell stood. He'd removed his Tibetan coat revealing a lean, taut torso contoured by a peach-coloured Calvin Klein T-shirt. "What's going on, Hank? You know how much money I owe?"

Others joined in, shouting about mortgages and rent.

Keegan looked over his shoulder checking the rear exit. He was about to go down as the man who'd lost them a quarter of their wage. He raised his hand to settle the racket, then introduced Wong.

The codeine tablets made Wong feel as if he was floating in a fish tank. That was bad. He'd made a tactical error. One did not enter battle on opiates. He should have marshalled his pain, filed it to a point, and used it like a lance. So he inhaled and stood, clasped his hands behind his back and scanned the crowd as if studying enemy lines through field glasses. Remembering his Toastmaster classes, he opened with a positive statement.

"You men bake the bread of the nation." He paused to let the glory of this fact gild their pride. "You get paid twenty dollars and twenty-five cents an hour. And," he added, before anyone could comment, "you deserve it. In fact, you deserve more." Wong watched the reaction move like a rumour of reprieve through the crowd.

"You're all intelligent men. You read the paper. You follow the dollar. Nineteen ninety-six has been one of the worst years for the dollar since the Depression. Canada is in crisis and so is Bestbuy." Wong observed the word *crisis* register upon their faces. "Question: if any of you ran a business that lost money, what would you do? I'll tell you—you'd make changes. That's what we have to do. Make changes." Wong took a breath. "You've had a week to consider the offer. I know it's sudden. But it's legal. Hank can assure you of that." He glanced at Keegan, but of course there was no support to be found there. Wong faced the bakers again, then plunged the lance to the bone. "Back East is prepared to close the doors unless you accept the wage cut. Five-twenty-five an hour." Wong sat.

In the silence that followed, Mutton stepped up onto a chair. "Here ye be, lads. All ye've got to do now is drop yer drawers, bend over, and say thank you. And it won't be the first time. Hey Keegan, d'ye remember how we lost the Canadian Seaman's Union? No? I do. I were there. Nineteen forty-nine. Worldwide strike. Pickets around the globe. That were the headline. Best union this country ever had. And the Canadian govern-ment scuttled it. Let the Americans take over. Bloody helped them take over. They were in cahoots. Got Hal Banks and the SIU. Eight men shot dead by scabs on the Halifax docks. That's our so-called American brothers. That's our so-called Canadian government. Now they're doin' it to the bakers' union. You call it free trade, I call it rough trade, and you're the whore."

Keegan had to beat his shoe on the table to silence the uproar. For the next hour, he and Wong fielded accusations, answered questions, and quelled the racket. Finally, at nine-thirty, Keegan lifted the ballot box onto the table. "Prepare to vote."

§

When that lacrosse ball of bread whacked Wong on the back of the skull, his first thought was—blood clot— brought on by tension, lack of exercise, and too much pork. His vision blurred and he staggered. Then he understood why his vision had blurred—his glasses were on the sidewalk. He picked them up and discovered a scrape on the left lens. He also saw the lump of dough on the grass outside the hall.

"Nice shot. You got the courage to admit to it?"

"Maybe it fell from the sky," said Mutton. "Divine retribution."

Wong gazed a long time at Mutton, making a note of his face.

Mutton jumped to attention, clicking his heels and saluting. "Mutton, Scot F. Sir!"

Wong turned away and proceeded slowly, with deliberation and dignity, to his XJ7.

The vote had been YES. They'd take the cut and keep their jobs. There'd never been any choice and they all knew it.

Now Epp followed Klaus down the sidewalk. "It's like a off-ramp, Klaus. Now's the time to make the move."

Sometimes Klaus wished Epp would just go off somewhere and die. Klaus tried sounding as exasperated as possible. "Make the move with what? Fifteen an hour? You know how much capital it takes to start a business? It's over. Forget it." Klaus watched Epp's eyes open so wide the whites showed all around them. Ever since Klaus left graveyard, Epp's eyes had worn the perpetually hurt look of a betrayed child.

Despite wearing a fleece-lined jean jacket and a toque, Epp was trembling. "You think I'm gonna do graveyard the rest of my life? Why you think they call it graveyard anyway?"

The pleading in Epp's voice made Klaus walk faster. He stabbed at the door lock with his key, got it open, then looked at Epp, who was due at Bestbuy at eleven for his shift. "You're late for work."

CHAPTER TWO

A Plunge in the River

EPP REACHED BESTBUY at ten fifty-seven, just about the time Klaus was driving up the alley behind The Upper Crust with that can of gas. Epp pulled on his whites and punched his time card. Every Bestbuy employee had five pairs of white cotton pants and five white cotton shirts. In theory, these were supposed to fit, but anyone who fell outside the size range of the bulk-purchased uniforms had to make their own alterations. At a lean five-three, Epp had to roll up the sleeves and the pant cuffs, then borrow the stapler from the shipping desk to tighten the waist so the pants didn't droop. He was officially a janitor, but spent the first half of every shift out back dumping flour into the silo until the red light went on. As a result, every night Epp inhaled flour by the sackful. He'd been doing it twenty-two years, and worried that soon he'd be on one of those oxygen cylinders, wheezing with white lung, the baker's version of what miners got from breathing coal dust. After that it'd be straight to the boneyard.

At one hundred-and-twenty pounds, Epp was a runt; the flour sacks he dumped weighed forty kilos each. Epp didn't know exactly how much forty kilos was in pounds, but it was too much, it was dead weight, like shifting a corpse, or how he imagined shifting a corpse to be. But a corpse at least there'd be arms and legs to grab. The forty kilo sacks only had ears. That's what they called the corners, the points of paper Epp gripped when he heaved the sacks from the pallet to the flour-dump. The flour-dump was a chest-high vibrating sieve the size of a ticket booth. The flour got sucked through the sieve to the silos where it was stored. When Epp got home each morning, he coughed flour. He picked it from his nose, his ears, even dug it from his belly button. It went right through his pants and clung to his crotch like he was going grey down there. There was flour on his basement suite floor, his couch, his sheets, even in his coffee. Epp drank fifteen to twenty cups a day and lived on raisin bread he stole from work.

The bakery had grey cement floors, grey cement walls, and a twenty-five foot ceiling with track lighting.

There was a box of salt tablets by the drinking fountain, and a Worker's Compensation Board poster that pictured a wooden packing crate. The caption read: GEORGE TRIED LIFTING THIS BY HIMSELF. (THE CRATE'S DOING FINE.)

§

By three A.M. the bakery was silent. The bread waited in trays for the trucks and the overhead conveyors had been shut off. The silence felt like a lull in the world, a low-tide calm during which Epp and Dan Donnelly, the two janitors, dwelled on their private concerns. Epp thought of Lee. She'd dumped him five years ago, but he still thought of her every night. They'd been connoisseurs of flea markets and garage sales. She used to plan their entire weekend around them. When she got the table at the flea market on Terminal Avenue, Epp was thrilled, her own table, *their* own table. Epp was proud of being with Lee, proud that the other vendors knew them as a couple, and that he didn't have to pay the quarter to get in. He'd always bring her coffee, or spell her so she could step out for some air, because he worried about her lungs. After all, everything in the flea market was turning to dust. It was bad enough she smoked rollies without inhaling the dust of old books, crumbling couches, and rotting shoes. Everything there had that basement smell. That was something Epp didn't like, that and the men who looked at Lee. She sold leather belts and bags, plus a specialty line of leather panties and brassieres. You had to order those in advance. The guys'd always ask about them. They'd grin and ask if she was wearing them now, and could they see. Epp, all five-three of him—five-five in his Daytons—would feel the blood pumping up big in his ears.

"It's none'a your business what she's wearin'."

Lee looked hot in her black leather coat with the red fringe along the backs of the arms. She smelled good too, a rich sweet smell of fresh leather. Lee, on her part, had liked how Epp came home smelling of baked bread, even though he was only a janitor and not a real baker. And there was that time, his thirty-fifth birthday, when she buttered him, buttered him like a cob of corn. He'd never forget that birthday, especially since by the next one she was gone. She left because "they weren't going anywhere." Epp had asked where she wanted to go but she couldn't say, though she left on the back of a Harley.

And now his buddy Klaus was gone, too. They only saw each other when their shifts overlapped for an hour in the morning. Epp felt betrayed when Klaus left graveyard. He wanted onto day shift too, but Singh, the supervisor, wouldn't let him.

"Why not? I got the seniority."

Singh had told him why not: "Because you're a fuck-up."

Singh kept him tucked away on graveyard for his own good. But even there Epp screwed up. He got his hand flattened between the rollers of the moulder four years ago and it swelled to the size of a boxing glove. He nearly blew his eardrums out cleaning them with an airhose. He smashed his fingers on the iron bread racks at least once a year. And one time, when they let him load the oven, the mechanical arm that raked in the pans caught him and he got dragged in too. Klaus had hit the emergency stop button and they hauled Epp out by his feet, eyebrows gone and hair reduced to the fuzz on a coconut.

Epp knew they laughed at him. He heard them. Even when they weren't laughing he heard them. When he got his vintage 1974 Duster, they laughed because he'd had to nail blocks to the pedals so he could reach them. He still had a locket containing Lee's picture dangling from the rearview mirror along with a red garterbelt.

Getting back to the job, Epp dragged a sack from the pallet. He slit it lengthwise, then wrestled it onto the wire mesh where the flour got sieved through into the silos, except, that is, for the flour that puffed up in big clouds contributing to his white lung. And now they were down to fifteen bucks an hour. A thirty-five dollar a day cut. One-seventy-five a week. When he got home, he'd work out what it came to a year. He gutted another flour sack and heaved it onto the vibrating grate. The flour sacks came in boxcars. Five Roses Flour. After a night unloading one of those boxcars your fingers were shot, the tips bruised and bleeding like they'd been whacked with hammers. Epp slit open another one. Flour dusted his face. When Epp tried using white lung as a reason to get off graveyard, Singh had pointed out the box of disposable face masks right there next to the earplugs and gloves. But Epp didn't want to wear one of those gauze masks. Klaus always said it was too late for masks because they were all dead anyway. Epp had liked that. It sounded tough, and it was true: they were old guys now, let the kids wear masks, there was still hope for them. Thinking like that made Epp walk differently, like he'd just got laid, like he was an old campaigner, a veteran of the wars, a sod buster who'd been walking these goddamn cement floors since before some of these young jobbers were born. Epp even remembered when they used real eggs in the bread. They'd actually stood there cracking real eggs into buckets of flour.

Epp was forty, and tortured by the thought that he'd be on graveyard forever, or until the plant shut down, whichever came first. His only hope had been Big Klaus quitting and opening his own shop and hiring him, but now that was all shot to hell. Klaus was backing out. Epp, abandoned on graveyard, tore open another sack.

He thought of that oxygen cylinder awaiting him, an oxygen cylinder and a wheelchair, and no Lee. Unable to bear it, he turned and shouted at the cement walls: "THATS WHY THEY CALL IT GRAVEYARD SHIFT!"

Nothing.

The sacks of flour absorbed the sound. He was alone except for the discarded dough quietly bloating in rusty barrels on the loading dock. Fueled by yeast, the dough swelled until it overflowed and slopped to the floor. It was all going to waste, like his life. Epp looked around. There was the forklift. Epp had never driven the forklift. Twenty years and he'd never been allowed to drive it once. Singh wouldn't even let him sit in it and pretend.

Epp climbed on. The first thing he did was slam the forklift into the wall. Next, he backed up and hit the flourdump. Then he swung around the corner and found himself heading toward the edge of the loading dock and a five-foot drop.

Dan Donnelly, spraying insecticide along the walls, screamed: "EPP!"

Epp jumped off the forklift, but, having forgotten to put it in neutral, it ran straight over Donnelly's foot then glided off the dock.

§

Singh called the ambulance then cut Donnelly's boot from his foot. Donnelly's shirt was transparent with sweat and he was shrieking, beating the floor with his hand like a hit bird beating the ground with its wing.

When the ambulance left with Donnelly, Singh looked around and discovered Epp had vanished. Singh found him out back by the sinks where the machine parts got washed. He'd barricaded himself into a corner with stacks of blue plastic bread trays and armed himself with the power-washer, a pressurized hose that shot scalding water.

"Stay back!" Epp fired water over Singh's head to prove he meant business.

"Okay," said Singh. "Come out of there." And Singh, holding out his hand for the weapon, walked toward him.

Panicking, Epp gripped the lever and hit Singh square in the chest with a blast of hot water that knocked him on his ass.

Singh crawled back out of range and hid behind a drum of canola oil. His shirt was soaked. He considered calling Wong, then changed his mind given what Wong had been through at the union meeting. Donnelly had told Singh all about it. So he decided to wait until Klaus came in. Singh knew Epp and Klaus were buddies, that Epp had got worse without Klaus around to keep him in line. Singh shouted, "Epp. You wanna talk to Klaus?"

For a minute Epp said nothing, thinking it was a trick. But who else was there? Epp had even written Klaus into his will as beneficiary of his estate. Epp hadn't known he even had an estate until the lawyer explained it was only a fancy word they used to describe your stuff. Not that Epp had much stuff. There was his Duster, his barbells, his fish tank, his bird cage, and his moth collection. "Yeah! Get Klaus! I'll talk to Klaus!" And even as Epp spoke he felt his throat thicken with tears. He saw the cops on the TV news hunkered behind the open doors of their cars, waiting for the signal to storm the bakery and haul him out in handcuffs.

"Can you hold on?"

"Sure!" Now Epp felt better. He heard the concern in Singh's voice, like he cared, like they were working together on this, like Epp was in a bind and it wasn't his fault, not really. If Singh'd only let him drive the forklift once or twice this would've never happened. If they'd only let him off graveyard everything'd be fine. He checked his watch, the watch Lee had given him. Four-twenty A.M. Forty minutes before Klaus'd be in. Epp peered out at the sacks of flour and sugar, the boxes of Australian raisins, the barrels of canola oil that Klaus said was another name for rapeseed, the walk-in freezer that held the lard and the butter. He cupped his palm over his mouth and nose and breathed, imagining the oxygen cylinder waiting for him. White lung. He wondered if it'd hurt.

35

§

When Klaus plodded in at five A.M. Singh explained the situation. Klaus said nothing. He'd been up all night drinking, unable to sleep, going over and over what he'd done to The Upper Crust, reminding himself he'd been drunk, and, by extension, temporarily insane. He wondered how that would stand up in court. If they'd just stop pushing him maybe he'd open that goddamn shop. But they pushed, both Epp and Darlene pushed. Well that's what happened when you pushed. On the way to work he'd listened to the news. There was no mention of any arson attempt on a bakery. Klaus felt relieved. It was over. The owner would collect his insurance and that'd be it. Yet when he got to work and learned Epp had run over Donnelly with the forklift, guilt rose around Klaus like the water in a backed-up toilet.

He followed Singh out back and saw the wall of trays. At first he didn't know what to say, then he said, "Hey, Epp. What happened to all that beer?"

Epp watched from behind the trays. "Beer?" Klaus meant the beer Epp made in the green garbage can last summer. Epp and Klaus had sat sucking on that siphon hose like Turks sharing a hookah, the floor covered in bottles and caps and carboys and spilled corn sugar. Klaus had talked again about opening a bakery of his own and baking quality bread, not the white flour crud Bestbuy pumped out. And Epp had nodded yeah, yeah, getting all worked up, thinking it was really going to happen. Epp laughed now, remembering. "We drank it!"

"Did you get any in the bottles?"

"Sure! Some. It's still there!"

"Well, let's drink them."

Epp was weeping now, the hot tears softening the dried flour crusting his cheeks. He wished Klaus was still on graveyard with him. He wished they still met at The Blue Boy before work and downed a few fast ones. He wished Klaus still talked about their bakery, how they'd make their own hours, be their own boss, even get to know the customers. He and Klaus even used to shake hands like it was a done deal. Then they'd gulp their beers and head to work, always arriving just in time to punch in at eleven so Singh couldn't give them shit. And they'd be smiling, smiling like they knew things, like they had plans, inside information, like yeah, we're on graveyard shift all right, but fuck you, we're not dead yet.

"Okay. I'm comin' out." And, taking a big breath, Epp stepped from behind the wall of blue plastic bread trays.

§

While Klaus counselled Epp, Singh went to his office and called the ambulance again. He'd decided Epp had gone and had a nervous breakdown. Twenty minutes later, the same two guys who'd carried out Donnelly were escorting Epp to the door, maintaining a balance between brotherly concern and force.

"I said I'm okay. I don't wanna go nowheres. Tell 'em, Klaus."

"Epp, don't worry."

But when Epp spotted the morning shift guys all gathered to watch, he knew by their expressions that he was heading for the electric chair. The procession passed the coffee room and then reached the storage area, where plastic bread bags in boxes sat stacked to the ceiling. One attendant released Epp to open the zinc-plated door that led to the parking lot.

Klaus offered Epp his hand.

Seeing that hand extended so formally, Epp choked up. He'd thought they were going to let him go, that it was all right, that Singh and Klaus were on his side.

"You okay?"

"He's fine." The attendant used that professionally optimistic voice. "Just a little tired. Nights. I know what that's like." He looked to his partner holding the door.

The partner nodded on cue. "Sure. Make anyone crazy."

"I ain't crazy."

The attendants looked at each other.

Klaus tried to sound comforting. "Epp."

"I told you I ain't crazy."

"They're only talking."

"Good night's sleep you'll be fine," said the guy gripping his arm.

But Epp knew B.S. when he heard it. Unable to meet their eyes, he watched their boots. Klaus's boots were tan and scuffed and the seams lined with flour. He couldn't see the other guy, but the one holding him wore black shoes, shiny black shoes contrasting his white pant cuffs, and that said one thing: Institution. They were taking him away, to the funny farm, like that song, ha ha, hee hee, ho ho, except it wasn't funny. He thought of Diplock at the orphanage; he used to get Epp and put him in a sleeping bag, then sit on the opening and keep him in there. Epp would panic inside that hot felt pouch. He'd scream, but the padded bag would absorb his voice and he'd be certain he was going to die. Then Diplock would let him out and make Epp pay a dollar for saving his life.

Klaus still had his hand out to shake. Epp reached to take it, then wrenched free, ducked down the cement steps and sprinted out across the lot. The ambulance attendants swore then ran after him. The bakers followed, whooping and laughing and shouting encouragement.

"Epp! Left! Go left!"

"No! Right! Right!"

Epp glanced over his shoulder and saw six men, bakers and ambulance attendants, all in white pants and shirts, hard after him. They fanned out to corral him, like madhouse orderlies hunting an escapee. Scotty Mutton now arrived on the scene. Gliding into the lot in his Datsun 510, he joined the chase, honking and driving through the crowd, scattering them all like sheep. Epp ran like he'd run as a kid, head down in case they threw rocks. He'd always been running in those days, from dogs and cops and from guys who just didn't like his mug. He leaped across the railway tracks, hit the chainlink fence surrounding Weldwood, and bounced off. Trapped, he looked left, right, then cut back to the left.

"The river! He's going for the river!"

The attendants were back in the ambulance now, following the action like a TV news van. Bell, who ran four times a week, was gaining, while Mutton cruised alongside offering both advice and his flask of Seagrams.

"Longer stride, Epp lad. Head up and longer stride! Now you've got it."

Epp's steel-toed boots felt like clay pots on his feet and the air scored his throat like asbestos. He plunged straight through the scrub cottonwood along the bank and slapped into the river. Bell skidded and grabbed the trees to keep from going in. Singh and the others caught up. They watched Epp dog-paddle out and then the clay-grey current catch him. He was swept downstream toward a sawdust barge. When he hit the barge he groped along the black planking to an iron ladder, hauled himself out and fought his way up the sawdust like a desert fugitive climbing a dune. Spooked gulls screeled away as he reached the top, where, finally, he looked back, a small shape burnt into the aluminum sky of dawn. Above him, gulls spiralled and factory smoke rolled from the stacks.

"Epp!"

"Keep going!"

Klaus said nothing, just raised his hand signalling good luck, feeling, along with his guilt, a flicker of envy.

Epp actually started to wave, as if they'd come to see him off on his journey and he wanted to thank them all for their kind support. Yet he looked lost, like a refugee. Then, stepping back, he lost his balance, groped the air and disappeared down the other side. In one second all that remained were Epp's footprints, and the nick in the perfect ridge of sawdust where he'd stood.

"There!" Bell pointed to a speck bobbing off downstream.

"That's a log," said Singh.

"Is it?"

No one could tell for sure. They followed along the

bank until blackberry vines and old railroad ties blocked the way. They stared until Epp was out of sight down river between the log booms. Then they looked at each other. Now what? They couldn't just go back and start their shift. So they stood there, the full impact of what had just happened slowly registering on them. What also registered were the riverside smells of cottonwood, dandelion, silty water, and sawdust. It was 5:40 in the morning, spring in Vancouver, the April rain tapering off and the relentlessly optimistic trees in full flower once again.

Finally, Singh broke the mood. "Come on."

§

They crowded into Mutton's 510 and drove back to the bakery, arguing about calling the cops.

"Of course we have to call the cops." Singh headed for his office.

The rest returned to the coffee room like schoolkids going back to their desks after a fire drill. At least they had cops to look forward to. Cops. There hadn't been cops at the bakery since they dragged Stahl off for assaulting a hooker.

Stahl swung open the Kelvinator and squinted at the shelves stacked with tinned milk and abandoned lunch bags. He punched holes in a tin using the milk-glazed opener dangling from the grubby string.

Bell opened a baggie of carrot sticks. "You think he's dead?"

Scotty Mutton poured two-and-a-half inches of sugar into a cup then topped it up with coffee and joined them at the main table, bringing with him his smell of sperm and beer. "Naw." He eyed Bell and his carrot sticks. "Should eat more tripe. I like a good flap of tripe now and again. Tripe and kidney pie. Or liver and marmalade. Ye can't beat liver and marmalade for breakfast."

"I don't eat liver," said Bell. "I don't eat any meat, but I especially don't eat organ meat." Bell tossed a handful of flax seeds into his mouth then went at another carrot. He nodded at Mutton's cup. "All that sugar and caffeine's going to kill you."

Mutton grinned revealing teeth pitted at the gums. Mutton had the complexion of a freshly peeled scab. The scars above his eyes reflected a habit from his youth wherein he'd pried the caps off beer bottles with his brow ridge. Beneath these scars, however, his eyes were merry with a lifetime of jolly sodomy. He winked at Bell.

Bell turned to Klaus. "Was it the cutback?"

Klaus sat in silence at the other table. Three arborite tables furnished the lunchroom: the main table for the guys "on the floor," the smaller table for the office people "upstairs," and the third table, where Klaus sat alone.

43

Above him dead flies darkened the fluorescent light fixture. Beside him, a calendar featured a photograph of seed-studded loaves of 12-grain bread, the sort Bestbuy never baked. "Yeah. The cutback." Klaus thought of The Upper Crust. He also thought of the letters he'd written on the illiterate Epp's behalf. He'd sent the letters to both union and management. The letters were supposed to get Epp off graveyard and onto days. But Klaus had intentionally written them badly, making them ludicrous and incoherent. He didn't want Epp following him on to days, so he'd scuttled the little bugger. Now he felt like a puddle of vomit. "And graveyard. He wanted off graveyard. It causes depression. Bicameral disorder." Klaus had heard the term on the news.

Bell nodded. He knew the term from his psychology courses at school.

Stahl spat air. "Go home, Klaus."

After twenty years of working together, the animosity between Klaus Mann and John Sourdough Stahl had long been reduced to ritual. Klaus knew Stahl hated the fact that Klaus had a degree.

Bell said, "Where are those cops?" For the moment, young Bell-the-Buddhist had forgotten that he disapproved of cops.

"The White Spot eating their free burgers." Sourdough Stahl's hatred of cops had less to do with his having been hauled out of the bakery in front of every-

44

one, than with his having failed the police entrance exam. His bitter manner announced his view that everything in life was stacked against him. His voice hinted the anger of a man who believed he'd been cheated from day one. "It's Friday. They're slacking off."

"They got you fast enough," grinned Mutton.

Stahl's escapade with the cops would scar him for life. He figured that's why he didn't get offered the supervisorship that went to Singh three years back.

Klaus, meanwhile, said nothing. What mattered was that he had sixteen beer waiting in the Rabbit. He'd top up the three he'd drunk on the way to work with two more at each coffee break and three at lunch. This routine had resulted in a beer belly that now swelled from below his belt all the way up to his sternum, where, in his middle age, breasts were forming. Hairy breasts. He could cup them in his hands and jiggle them. When Klaus had first met Darlene he'd had a gut like a plank and could do fifty push-ups in one go.

Bell got up and went into the washroom. Stahl watched him, then turned to Klaus. "So, Klaus, when you opening up shop?" They all knew of Klaus's bakery plans. "Time to put your money where your ass is. And take Epp too." Stahl winked at the others, but no one smiled. "That is if he isn't belly-up down river."

The dozen bakers in the room became still.

Mutton said, "Christ, Stahl, yer a piece'a shite."

Stahl wished Mutton would go die from AIDS. He tried sounding innocent. "What?"

After a moment of seemingly deep consideration, Klaus forced himself to his feet, as if his two hundred and twenty pounds were three hundred and twenty, went to the Pyrex pot and poured himself another cup of the liquid carbon that passed for coffee. He wondered if anyone here knew The Upper Crust was for sale.

Stahl slouched back in his aggressive and leisurely fashion, crossed his legs, and bounced his foot. "Yeah," he drawled, "little fuck's probably fish food by now. All he was good for anyway."

Klaus turned.

Everyone waited.

Fear spread inside Klaus like poison ivy. Once again he saw Epp cowering behind those trays, he saw Epp in the river, and he saw the letters he'd written on Epp's behalf, letters that all this time Epp believed were pleading his case. Klaus tossed that hot coffee straight into Stahl's crotch.

CHAPTER THREE

Into the Oven

STAHL DECIDED AGAINST slashing Klaus's tires because it'd be too obvious. He glanced down: it looked like he'd wet himself. Besides being production foreman, Stahl ran the moulders, which rolled the flattened doughs into loaves then dropped them into greased pans. Bestbuy's machinery was fifty years old, shipped out from England after World War II, immense iron dinosaurs scabbed with rust. The machines were already out of date back when Stahl first started. Now, in 1996, they were ancient. Despite fans, the oven kept the bakery so hot that even in winter their sweat-soaked shirts sucked their backs, and their paper hats dissolved on their heads.

47

One hand across his crotch, Stahl went to the divider, the machine that cut the four hundred pound mother dough into loaves, and stood so he could watch Bell without being seen. Bell was on pans, loading them end-to-end onto the belt, and he was sweating so much he shone under the fluorescent lighting as if he'd been oiled. It was the hottest part of the bakery there where the iron pans were stacked in long high rows straight from the oven. Bell's T-shirt was sealed tight to his torso. Stahl watched Bell wipe his face with a handkerchief. Stahl didn't know anyone who carried a handkerchief. Most guys just used their sleeve or the end of their shirt, even the women who worked out on shipping. Stahl didn't even own a handkerchief. He figured he and Bell were the same height. John Stahl was six-foot-one, but bad posture reduced him to five-foot-nine. His habit of pulling his head down between his shoulders made him look like he was perpetually expecting a clout across the ear. He had large hands, but narrow shoulders, and here again his posture came into play. Stahl's shoulders looked like coathangers. Watching Bell, Stahl leaned his hip against one of the machines, feeling the vibration rumbling alongside his groin, and thought of that Magic Fingers bed in the motel on Kingsway and the transvestite.

Stahl had picked him up at Quebec Street and 3rd. He knew Vancouver's three whore runs. The low-track was north of Hastings near the waterfront, the high-track was downtown, and mid-track was Quebec Street. From half a block away Stahl knew by the hips it was a tranny. After circling the block checking for cops, Stahl pulled alongside. The tranny was Filipino, about five-five, with huge eyes rimmed with gold make-up. Stahl was so terrified he couldn't talk. A john with the jitters was nothing new, so the tranny climbed right on in and fastened the shoulder strap, taking care not to wrinkle his leopard skin top. That struck Stahl as incredible, a whore doing up her-his seatbelt. He put the van in gear and pulled out, blood banging like a bell in his skull. It occurred to him he should ask the price, bargain, nego-tiate, but he didn't know where to begin, and was too scared to try, so he drove. He got onto Main, then Kingsway, and headed out past the Vietnamese and Korean strip malls toward a motel he knew. His heart was beating so hard he actually worried he might have a heart attack, or a stroke. One, he knew, was worse than the other. But which? He considered asking the tranny, then thought it would sound weird.

They got stuck at the red light at Kingsway and Victoria. Stahl stared straight ahead. He could smell her-his perfume. It smelled good, like flowers.

"My name's Margarita."

"John."

She-he laughed. "Okay."

It took Stahl a moment to get it: John, john. He was a *john*.

"You look tired . . . John."

The light changed. "Long day." From the corner of his eye, Stahl saw him-her looking around the van. He had five loaves of Ovenjoy Brown in the back. He'd stashed them out by the dumpster then picked them up after his shift.

"You a baker?"

Stahl panicked. "Me? No. Just, you know, was a sale."

The motel was a semicircle of stucco bungalows dating from the 1940s. The sleepy East Indian running the place was watching a rerun of *The Man from U.N.C.L.E.* Stahl paid for the room and returned to the van where Margarita sat waiting. They had number three. He pulled into the parking spot.

"Ooh, looks cozy."

Stahl saw that it did. A little house with a curtained window, a flower box, shrubs, even a mail slot in the door. Margarita plucked the key from Stahl's fingers and led the way. Once inside, she-he went into the bathroom and turned on the shower. Stahl looked around. The place smelled musty, and the floorboards shifted loosely under the indoor-outdoor carpet. The gold bedspread had those tufts all over it. His parents had had one like it. There was a word for those tufts. On the wall hung a painting of a farmyard done all in shades of blue.

The water stopped. Stahl turned as Margarita stepped from the bathroom in a sequined bikini, carrying a jug of Mazola oil. Stahl felt his pants tighten across his zipper.

Margarita's attention jumped to the bed. "Got a quarter?"

Stahl hadn't noticed the control panel and coin slot. He reached into his pocket.

Margarita said, "Let me." And her hand slid in along his groin, but it wasn't a quarter she found.

Eventually they got the bed going. The motor in the mattress was muted and the vibration felt like a power drill against your palm. Margarita stood up on the mattress and began a belly dance. She stepped closer to Stahl, raised her arms over her head, and said, "Take them off."

Stahl didn't expect to think of Jesus Christ on the cross at that moment. But that's what came into his head—Jesus Christ, with that loincloth that always looked like it was about to slip down. Stahl watched himself reach out, eyes hot and prickling as if he was about to weep, his pulse panicking in his throat, and nausea churning his stomach. Margarita stopped moving and offered her pelvis so he could catch hold. He slid his fingers between her hot belly and the taut elastic. It was moist and mossy; her sweat salted the sweetness of her perfume.

"Deeper."

Stahl hesitated.

"Go on."

Stahl obeyed. Chenille. The word was *chenille*.

§

Stahl had run two red lights before he saw the blood on his knuckles. Beneath the blood were tooth marks. Rabies. Stahl had heard somewhere that human saliva could cause rabies. She-he was a lot older than he'd realized. Mid-thirties, maybe even forty. It was the lines at the corners of her eyes cracking the gold make-up that betrayed her, that and the lack of surprise when he punched her: she just stared up at him with a look of weary disappointment.

Over the weekend Stahl's hand improved, but Monday morning he still had a bandage on it when he went to work. The cops arrived about ten. Stahl figured the tranny must've got his licence plate number. The cops cuffed Stahl and escorted him to the door. He never said a word, then or later. The bakers, however, imagined all manner of scenario, presenting each one to Stahl at the lunch table as if it was a guessing game. Stahl just stared at the newspaper, or went outside and sat in his van. A week or so later Mutton confronted him in the parking lot after work, and narrated everything that had happened, including the detail about the vibrating bed.

"I know her, Stahly."

Stahl's glance kept cutting toward the bakery door to see if anyone was watching.

"I ain't told no one. Not yet anyway."

"Whataya want?"

"A ride home."

Stahl had stared like his ears were faulty.

"Ye heard me. Car's in the shop."

They were at Main and 50th, Little India, when Mutton pulled his flask from his black sports coat. It was his tin flask. He had them in pewter, plastic, onyx, and even a silver plated one from Bangkok that had a matching opium pipe. He tipped the flask toward Stahl offering a drink. Stahl shook his head. Mutton's Adam's apple bobbed as he drank. As he refitted the cap he became reflective. "D'ye remember the night we drank the cough syrup, Sourdough?"

"Don't call me Sourdough."

"Burton Brothers Throat Balm, 22% alcohol, fortified with codeine."

"No."

"No?" Mutton shook his head in bemusement. "John Sourdough Stahl. Ye're really in the closet, aren't ye."

53

"The fuck're you talkin' about?"

"I'm sayin' I never forget a vintage."

Stahl said nothing. He remembered. It was twenty-three years ago. July, 1973. Mutton had only recently left the merchant marine at the time, so spoke mainly of the ports he'd visited. Mutton had actually been to Africa and South America and India. And he had pictures, so Stahl, with thoughts in those days of maybe going to sea himself, went to Mutton's apartment one night after work. He saw the pyramids, Sancta Sophia, and the Blue Mosque, plus a few other things that he, at the age of twenty-one, had never seen before, things that sobered him right up despite the Burton Brothers Throat Balm.

"Did I ever tell ye about the brothels in Iraq?"

Stahl drove in silence.

"All the doors on the right are lasses, all the doors on the left, lads." As they passed through Little India, Mutton watched the saried women going in and out of the shops. "The lads sit on pegs to keep their arses primed for action."

Stahl shouted, "I thought he was a woman, okay, a woman!"

Mutton looked at him calmly. "Well he is, Stahly, he is."

§

Lurking behind the moulder, Stahl continued watching Bell. He figured Bell could be on TV. He had that look—everything perfect—hair, teeth, complexion, and a belly like a board. He even smelled good when he sweated. Stahl knew because he inhaled whenever Bell passed by. Bell was beautiful. Stahl, in contrast, looked like a mug shot. He could shower in the morning and by noon his hair was lank with oil. He had sensitive skin, so shaved only every second day, which meant he was always grubby with stubble. Years ago he'd tried growing a beard, but it looked like rat fur. What he really wanted to do was dye his hair blonde. But there was no way. He could just hear these bastards in the bakery laughing at him. If he ever moved, though, that'd be the first thing he'd do, dye his hair blonde. He wondered what kind of underpants Bell wore.

When Clyde Graves, the day shift supervisor appeared, Stahl hid his coffee-stained crotch by pressing it against the rounder, the machine that tumbled the doughs in flour so they didn't stick. He watched Graves making with that disapproving Presbyterian squint as he observed the moulders. He knew what Graves was thinking: too fast, the moulders were running too fast. Stahl edged over and turned the brass crank slowing the belt.

Graves nodded across at Stahl, meaning good move, good eye, wise stewardship. Stahl knew Graves viewed the bakery in religious terms. God was above, then the angels, then the supervisors, while below them were the foremen, and then the men on the shop floor. To rise from foreman to supervisor was equal to achieving semi-divine status. Graves believed the supervisor occupied the role of intercessor between union member and upper management, between mortals and the American owners of Canada Bestbuy, those exalted males with faces of fire and voices like Jehovah.

Now Clyde Graves joined Stahl at the divider and noted down the exact number of units they'd run of the previous variety, 24-ounce Ovenjoy Brown. Graves was a stickler for measurement. He had a blood pressure kit in his car and tested himself three times a day. Graves had mastered his blood pressure problems by saying no to alcohol and yes to The Bible.

"Young Stahl! Thought any more about coming to church? What else you gonna do Sunday morning? Good a place as any to wear off your hangover." Graves, a reformed alcoholic, winked like a worldly man. He had a head like a scabbed apple and often came to work without his teeth. After writing down the production figures with a brand new HB pencil, Graves leaned closer, voice husky with innuendo, "Lotta single ladies sitting in those pews."

Crotch to the rounder, Stahl jumped a grin to his face implying he liked the sound of that. Then he changed the topic. "Hear about last night?"

Clyde Graves grew troubled. He shook his head, meaning sad, sad. "But better fifteen dollars an hour than no dollars an hour."

"How 'bout Epp?"

Now Graves looked really troubled. "I don't think Wong's going to be happy hearing about that. No sir. Singh's sticking around to tell him what happened. Were you there?"

Fear soured Stahl's stomach. "No. I mean yeah. I mean, I saw when they were haulin' him out. Just run off."

"You know what it is, don't you?"

Mesmerized by the glare on Graves's lenses, Stahl couldn't tell whether that was an accusation or a question.

Graves answered for him. "Man's been on graveyard too long."

"Well, sure. Causes depression. Bicameral disorder."

Graves nodded like that was exactly right. Then he winked. "'Course the little bugger's lucky to have a job."

"Well, yeah." Stahl nodded vigorously. Then he shook his head.

Graves slugged Stahl on the shoulder and walked off, frowning furiously and whistling cheerfully at the same time. He caught Scotty Mutton from behind and pretended to stab him repeatedly in the kidney with that long yellow pencil, then waved to Bell.

Stahl liked that Graves called him Young Stahl. It was better than Sourdough. He stepped away from the rounder and discovered he had a hard-on. He pressed up against the metal again, but the vibrating wheel tumbling those doughs made it worse, or better. Stahl's eyes bounced about like pool balls hunting holes to hide in. He saw Bell had pulled his shirt up now to cool his stomach. He'd pulled it up high, like a bra.

§

On his first break, Stahl went out to his van and called Keegan. As expected, Stahl got the answering machine, so he left a brief account of Epp's disappearance and then locked his cell back in the glove box. Taking his coffee from the dash, where it was steaming the glass and raising images of sex-misted windows, Stahl thought again of Bell. He glanced down at that coffee stain in his crotch. He would've changed his pants, but it was Friday and Nelsons had picked up their whites. Monday they'd be back, five freshly laundered sets.

Directly across from his van sat Bell's peach-coloured Karmann Ghia. Sometimes Bell showed up wearing a one-piece ski suit with zippers. Thinking of that ski suit, Stahl shut his eyes and imagined the sound of zippers slowly opening, and the rustle of relaxing nylon. He groaned. Then someone whacked his door.

"One-twenty over eighty!" Graves gave the thumbs up. "You swim?"

"Swim?" The thought of exposing his body in public horrified Stahl.

"You should swim. Get that ticker moving. Beat the stress. I swim three times a week and then do a hundred-and-twenty crunches. Look." Graves stood sideways showing Stahl his belly. "Flat. My mother's eighty-four and she walks up to the supermarket every morning and by golly she gives those cashiers heck." Graves laughed in pride, then became reflective. Stahl knew what was coming. "I knew your father from the old Weston's. Best dough man I ever worked with. These guys today." Graves shook his head, lamenting the passing of The Golden Age of mass-production baking. At least once a month Graves stated that he'd known Stahl's father, and Stahl always pretended to be hearing it for the first time. "How is he?"

"Great," lied Stahl.

"You're damn right he is." Graves gazed off toward the freezer trucks across the road at Betcher's Meats. "No sign of Epp?"

Stahl glanced around as if Epp might be on his way back at that very moment. "Nope."

Graves winked. "Little bugger's probably bobbing around out there in the chuck right now. End up in Bella Coola."

Stahl took his cue to laugh.

Graves became solemn. "This is just between us, but Epp's been writing letters asking to get off graveyard for almost a year now. If he goes and drowns the union'll get hold of it and believe you me they won't let go. Especially with that pay cut. Our friend Keegan'll be down here toot-sweet raking up all kinds of muck. Get my drift?"

Stahl nodded.

"We don't want this getting out of hand."

Stahl shook his head.

"You know what'll happen if it does."

Stahl didn't, but nodded anyway.

"Good. Got Donnelly in the hospital, a thirty-thousand dollar forklift belly up out back, and a man maybe drowned. Whose fault is it?"

Stahl felt himself catching on. "Singh?"

Graves nodded. "He was the Supervisor."

"His responsibility."

"Darn right." Graves's voice now took on a new tone. "You know I recommended you." Graves referred to the supervisorship that had come open three years earlier.

"Yeah, and they took Singh."

"Well, they just might send him back."

"Whataya mean?"

"Young Singh's gonna swing." Graves hoisted himself by an imaginary noose and Stahl got the picture.

Stahl thought of one word: supervisor. The company would sew blue crests onto all five of his work shirts.
He'd go from an hourly wage to a monthly salary. John
Stahl: supervisor. Graves had two years to retirement
and Stahl was already preparing himself. Next
Wednesday was the final session of Business Management I: Theory & Practice, and this time around he
meant to pass. Last semester, Stahl had sat in class feeling like dog dirt on white shag. There'd been a Chinese
guy named Jerome in the class. Stahl thought that was
a weird name. There was Harry Jerome, the black sprint-
er who took Bronze in Tokyo in the 100, and Jerome
the Giraffe on *The Friendly Giant*, but a Chinese Jerome?
Stahl gave him a ride home one night. Jerome planned
to open a cigar store. He'd been doing market research.
He'd been to Cuba talking to suppliers and even had a
business card. He also had samples, and that night on
the way home he'd lit one up, a Monte Cristo, and
passed it over saying, "Taste it, John." And Stahl did,
his hand trembling as he held it to his lips and sucked
on the thick dark end that was all wet and warm and
musky. They passed it back and forth like a reefer and
Stahl tried staying calm. He hadn't smoked a cigar since
he was ten years old, and stole a pack of wine-dipped
Tiparillos from Rosencko's Groceteria. Jerome, meanwhile, moaned as he smoked, as if he was getting a back
rub. He settled deeper into the van's seat and sipped the

cigar like it was wine. Jerome looked thirty, had eyes thin as papercuts, a ponytail, and wore cologne. He offered Stahl a drink when they reached his apartment.

"I gotta be up at five for work."

"In the *morning*?" Jerome's lidded eyes had widened in horror.

Driving home that night, Stahl had kept his left hand on the wheel and his right on the seat, where he could feel Jerome's body heat under his palm.

Sitting in his van in the bakery parking lot talking to Graves, Stahl got gloomy. "'Course it don't mean nothin' now. Place is finished." He did nothing to disguise the petulance in his voice. As far as he was concerned, it was all a conspiracy. Anonymous and evil men were Back East and down in the States, seated behind desks and in boardrooms, plotting against him with while-collared malice.

Graves got as severe as a schoolmaster. "This place is finished when I say so."

Stahl liked that. He became puppyish with enthusiasm. "I'm just finishing up that Business Management course I was telling you about."

"That's good. That's good." Graves nodded, then he leaned to look at Stahl's crotch. Stahl opened his legs wide. "Klaus Mann do that?"

"Yeah! Just went and did it."

Graves pressed his lips tight. "My blood pressure

doesn't need that sort of business. No sir. I'm going to have to have a talk with our Mr. Mann." Graves nodded again like that was a solemn promise.

When Graves was gone, Stahl got his cell phone out of the glove box and called Keegan back. This time he got him. "It's me."

"Who?"

Stahl felt insulted. He phoned the office three or four times a week, but Keegan never recognized his voice. Stahl suspected Keegan did it on purpose. "Me. Stahl."

"I got your message."

"Well there's more." Stahl told Keegan what Graves had said about Epp and the letters.

"Uh huh."

Uh huh? That was it? Uh huh? "So you know?"

"'Course I know." Then Keegan relented. "But that's good, John. Keep it up. I need you there, you know that. I need a good man on the inside."

"So . . . how's it look?" Stahl knew Keegan knew what he meant: what were his chances of getting a job in the union office. For years Stahl had been at Keegan to use his leverage and get him nominated for treasurer, but Keegan kept putting him off.

The sound of Keegan lighting a cigarette and inhaling deeply came through the phone. "After last night? Can't even think about it. Not now, anyway." He took

another drag. "Look. I'll be down in a couple of hours."
He hung up.

Stahl stared at his cell phone. Keegan always made it
sound like they had a special connection, like it's you and
me, like Stahl was his man, then he couldn't recognize
his voice. Union or management. Stahl was covering all
angles. He'd take whichever came his way. Of course who
knew, if a supervisor position opened up they'd probably
offer it to Klaus again. Maybe this time around he'd go
for it. Turning down the supervisorship had given Klaus
status in the union. Stahl figured Klaus had mental
problems. If Stahl got to be supervisor he'd do something about it, like stick Klaus back on graveyard or get
him laid off. And he'd bounce Epp out altogether. He'd
make changes. He'd paint the rollers on the moulder and
the pan-o-mat orange, so guys didn't get their hands
caught. He'd lobby for staggered wages so jobbers got
cut back to half pay. Stahl was long overdue. He was
forty-four. Twenty-eight years he'd worked in the bakery.
He knew every job from janitor to mixer to running the
slicers, yet Singh got promoted to supervisor ahead of
him. Singh had a degree in political science. What the
hell did political science have to do with running the
bakery that supplied half the supermarkets in B.C.? And
what was he going to do if they really did shut the doors
here? Go across the street to that meat plant? Drive a
cab? Stahl had been at Bestbuy since he was sixteen.

What did he have to show? A dozen RRSPs. Twelve lousy grand. How long would that last what with him supporting his old man? Stahl was forking out eleven hundred a month to top up his father's pension to keep him in a decent rest home.

What with more and more bread coming up from Seattle each night, threatening to put them all out of work, Stahl had done something desperate last week, something he'd never done before, something he'd always sneered at: he'd gone into an E.I. office and checked the job board. It hadn't been easy for someone who'd always worked. When he'd arrived, he'd lingered near the door ready to turn and leave. He'd watched Chinese and East Indian kids leading their parents through the process of filling out forms. He saw people standing in lines holding numbers, people standing near the walls, people sitting on chairs jingling keys to divert their crying kids, people standing at computer terminals. Computers. Stahl knew nothing of computers. He couldn't even make the ones on display in the stores do anything. He'd move the mouse right and the arrow would slide left. And those salesmen going on about RAM and ROM and megs and gigs. Goddamn con artists. He scanned the E.I. office for the job board. He always remembered guys at the bakery saying there were job boards with cards pinned to them, but all he saw was a poster titled:

ADVICE FOR JOB INTERVIEWS
1. Don't smoke
2. Don't bring a friend
3. Don't cross your arms or legs
4. Be relaxed

Outside, the rain was hitting so hard it bounced on the sidewalk. Inside, the wet coats and running shoes stank of anxious animals. When Stahl finally stepped off the mat, one foot skated on the puddled lino and he nearly fell. No one laughed, but a fat woman shouted: WHEE! and mimicked the way Stahl's leg had shot out. She wore soccer boots and had a tattoo on her shin. She pointed to her cleated boots.

"I don't take no chances. No way, not no more. I hit the deck up in Rupert at the fish plant and broke my elbow. Look." She pushed up her Montreal Canadiens jersey and showed the scarred and swollen joint. Then she demonstrated the crackling noise that came from her elbow when she moved it. "Hear that? All my cables're fucked up." Her brown-rooted blonde hair was held in a ponytail with a twist tie, black mascara ran in ghoulish streaks from the corners of her eyes, and her white sweat pants were pushed up to her knees. Her soccer boots were the old fashioned style, with the steel toe-cap. Stahl edged off in the other direction, but she sent her conversation right after him, talking louder the

farther away he went. "YEAH, I WAS ON COMPO FOR A
YEAR. THAT WAS HOW I GOT ADDICTED TO COKE.
THEY SAY IT MAKES YOU CRAZY, BUT I NEVER WENT
CRAZY ONCE. THEN WHEN I WENT TO REHAB I WENT
CRAZY FOUR TIMES. FIGURE THAT OUT. NOW I'M LIV-
ING WITH MY FRIEND CHANTAL. YOU KNOW CHANTAL?
SHE'S DOIN' HER GRADE 12. SHE'S GONNA GO TO UNI-
VERSITY NEXT YEAR, 'CAUSE SHE'S STATUS, EH, AND
IT'S LIKE FREE FOR HER. THEN WE'RE GOIN' BACK UP
TO RUPERT OR MAYBE LOS ANGELES 'CAUSE SHE MET
THIS BLACK GUY NAMED MONTEL."

When Stahl finally got too far away, she turned to
an elderly Sikh woman next to her and carried right on.
"I mean I'm not prejudiced, but he treats her like shit,
and when I said something he called me a fat bitch!"

On the far side of the room now, Stahl stared at one
of the computer screens, then at the keypad, then the
screen again. Next to him, a Chinese kid hit a number
and a long narrow printout unfurled from the slot like
a bank receipt. All down the row people worked the terminals. Stahl squinted at the screen.

1: Job List

He reached out with one hesitant finger and pressed
1. The screen went blank. Thinking he'd broken it, he
turned to get out of there quick, but it came back.

1) School bus driver: $8.00/hr.
2) Delivery driver: $7.00/hr.

67

3) Phone sales: $7.50/hr.

4) Drycleaning trainee: $7.25/hr.

Drycleaning. Stahl knew one thing about drycleaning—you ended up retarded. The chemicals melted your brain. And for seven-and-a-quarter an hour? Twelve hundred a month less tax? He'd be lucky to see eight-fifty. His rent alone was seven. He went through the list to the end, one hundred and twenty-seven jobs, and found only one related to baking.

Apprentice, Chinese bakery: $7.00/hr.

He hit the number 2 for Further Details: Must be willing to work graveyard.

He was about to leave when the crazy woman took the Chinese kid's place next to him.

"I gotta get me one of these things. You know, computer graphics, Internet. I was doing phone sales but the guy I was working for, he fuckin' fucked off and I didn't get paid. Now I'm back to square one and I can't type no more 'cause it hurts my elbow. I mean I was a good typer in high school. Chantal said I should do some acting. They're always after extras here. They call Vancouver Hollywood North, eh. And what they need, see, what they need is people like me, you know, regular people. Like you, you could prob'ly be the bartender or the cop or maybe the Bulgarian terrorist. I knew a Bulgarian up in Rupert named Jerko or Janko. I figure I could be Roseanne's sister, right. I just need fifty bucks for pictures 'cause you gotta have a portfolio to give the agency and then they call you up and mostly you just stand around and eat sandwiches. Hey, maybe we can go together. I know a photographer who owes me. We could prob'ly get a cut-rate." She leaned to look at the listing on Stahl's screen. "Graveyard. I wouldn't work graveyard. Fucks up your head."

§

When Stahl's coffee break was over, he went into the washroom and came face-to-face with Bell. The smell of Bell's cologne curled across Stahl's face sugaring the dank stink of the plumbing.

"Excuse me, John." Bell stepped past, brushing Stahl's shoulder.

Stahl turned and watched him walk toward the WASH YOUR HANDS BEFORE HANDLING BAKERY PRODUCTS sign on the door, and endured the panic of a man in the last scene of a movie watching the love of his life disappear forever. "Mutton let you go?" He flinched at the angry burr that habitually edged his voice.

Bell turned as though the question merited a long and considered response. His hairline was perfect, and though it was barely April he already had a tan. His shirt was tucked in now, his jeans were faded across his skier's thighs, and Stahl could see the bulge Bell's keys made in his pocket. Bell's jeans didn't have a zipper but buttons. "Yes." He waited for Stahl's next question, but Stahl just stared, so Bell reached for the door.

"Ski?"

Bell let go of the door. "Yes." Then, polite, he asked, "Do you?"

"Me?" Stahl sounded shocked. "No. Once. Only had the poles, though."

"You skied without skis?"

Stahl didn't know whether to laugh or be humiliated. But Bell smiled so Stahl did too.

"Had my workboots. Soles were bald so you know, was okay." Stahl tried thinking of something more to say. Had Bell ever dyed his hair blonde?

"Well." Bell went out.

That was the thing about Bell, he spoke properly, he always said Yes, never Yeah, and always called you respectfully by your first name. Did Bell know they called Stahl 'Sourdough'? Bell had only been at Bestbuy a year. The first time he showed up for a shift, Stahl recognized him. Then he realized from where—underwear ads. Bell modeled underwear. Stahl had Bell's picture, clipped from a catalogue and hidden in the wall of his apartment, along with dozens of others. Too embarrassed to buy a *Playboy*, much less anything more risqué, Stahl relied, like a thirteen-year-old, on catalogues from Sears and The Bay.

As for Bell, underwear ads had paid his way through a year of acting lessons, and his looks got him an agent. The pinnacle of his career was a commercial for lawn fertilizer. After that, he was reduced to crowd scenes. A year of depression followed, then a case of anal warts, a brush with Scientology that lost him all his friends and the last of his money, and finally he ended up working part-time at Bestbuy, and enrolled part-time at U.B.C. taking religious studies and psychology. He knew Stahl watched him. That worried him, but it intrigued him too. He liked being watched, and was not above pulling up his shirt and exposing his corrugated belly, or shoving a tea bun down his pants to enhance his bulge. Bell hated the bakery. It stank of stale sweat, and the flour dust clogged his pores. Between his psychology courses and mindless hours slinging pans, he plotted ways of snagging a sugar daddy. He wanted someone along the lines of a Belmondo or Mastroianni, with a Paris apartment or Tuscan villa, though he'd settle for someone with a sailboat or a condo at Whistler, or even someone who'd pay off his VISA bill. He kept his eye on the profs at U.B.C., gliding the halls like a glinting lure, visiting them with well-rehearsed questions on sexual aberration and the criminal mind.

When Bell was gone, Stahl stepped into the toilet and scrutinized everything. The graffiti gouged into the walls described the sexual practices of Clyde Graves and altar boys. A cartoon, sorry in its draftsmanship, showed Singh on his knees fellating Wong. Then Stahl sucked air so hard it stung the cavities in his eye teeth. STALL SUCKS THE SHIT OUT OF DEAD GOATS. That was new. New since yesterday. Stahl analyzed the handwriting. Klaus? Mutton? Pencil. It was in pencil. He reeled paper from the roll, soaked it in the sink, and then wiped away the pencilled words. The bastards. And they always spelled his name wrong.

§

Back on the shop floor, Stahl spotted Graves and Klaus sharing a good one by the oven. Stahl stepped behind the racks of bread waiting to be loaded and tried to listen, but the machine roar drowned their voices. He tried reading their lips, but all he saw was a lewd pantomime of jerks and gestures. Graves finished up by slapping Klaus on the shoulder. Then, clipboard tucked up tight under his arm, he whistled his way toward the office.

Stahl emerged from behind the racks and stood before the oven's mouth, feeling the scorching temperature tightening the skin across his face. He stared deep into the ferris wheel of slowly turning shelves. The oven held fifteen hundred loaves. The flames of the gas heat receding in rows along the sides made Stahl think of a torch-lit cave descending into Hades.

CHAPTER FOUR

The Bread Begins to Burn

TWO HOURS AFTER SINGH CALLED THEM, the cops still hadn't shown. The bakers began to fear they'd been robbed of the drama they so richly deserved. The mood in the coffee room became a toxic fuel of sullen excitement awaiting a matchstick. A trucker from Seattle provided it. So far, he'd succeeded in being unobtrusive by keeping his head down and staring at his waybills. Then Mutton arrived and turned everyone's attention to the foreigner.

"There he is, there he is," sang Mutton, striding in and heading for the coffee pot. "One of our American brothers drawn by the smell of blood'n money."

Stahl, desperate to redeem himself after letting Klaus

get away with tossing that coffee into his crotch, said, "Hey, scab."

The driver was big and burly, but pretended not to hear.

Stahl leaned forward. "Hey, scab."

Continuing to stare at his waybills, the driver said, "If your country's goin' down the tubes, it's 'cause you're lazy, over-unioned whiners."

That shocked everyone in the room.

"You're stealing our jobs."

The driver looked up. "Yer lucky we don't take yer goddamn country."

Stahl got scared. He and the driver were about the same size. "Oh yeah?"

"Just move the border north." The driver shifted his coffee cup forward, demonstrating how easy it would be.

"Fuck you."

The driver stood.

Stahl reared back gripping the table edge.

"I got work to do." And the driver headed for the door.

"Asshole."

The driver stopped, came over to the table and leaned on it. "I'm a asshole when I wanna be a asshole. But you're a asshole 'cause you is."

Before anything could go further, Mutton began telling the story of a cargo of sheep they once carried from Perth to Madras. "The crew were mostly Filipino and Tamil. The captain a Scot." Mutton winked. "It were the duty-free rum that did it, that and the tropical night. The captain performed a marriage ceremony, and the next morning a boozy Tamil bugger named Joseph Da Gama woke beside a trussed ewe. Above his bunk we'd hung wedding photos and cards of congratulations." Mutton paused to point out that Da Gama was a devout Catholic, so accepted his lot as God's will. "Was only when he discovered the wee sheep was no a virgin that he sued for annulment."

§

Klaus loaded the oven and thought of Epp floating in the river. He also thought of last night, the broken window, the gas, the whoof of the flames. Once again he reassured himself that it was a victimless crime, no one was hurt, and the owner would collect the insurance. He concentrated grimly on his job, working his way down the rack from the top shelf to the bottom, laying the pans gently onto the belt because one bump and the doughs—as pale and delicate as infants—would deflate with a yeasty sigh. On average, he loaded fifteen thousand loaves a day. He knew the Seattle plant could do double that because the oven was loaded automatically, straight from the proof box. Everything down there was new and automated. Vancouver Bestbuy hadn't advanced past the 1950s. Klaus also understood that the peak days of organized labour were done. It was no longer Us versus Them. It was Me versus You.

He worked until the belt was full, then he got a six-second rest to wipe his forehead, hoist his pants, and check the clock.

He ignored the clock as much as possible, so that when he did glance up a satisfying chunk of time had passed. With his brain submerged in beer, Klaus could sometimes load twenty minutes without surfacing. That felt good, that gave him a satisfying sense of progress through the shift, a sense of movement vital to his soul, given he stood stuck to a rubber mat seven hours a day performing a function no more complex than the opening and closing of a hinge. Klaus wished he could remove his frontal lobe and leave it in a jar of sugar water at the bakery door, then put it back in on the way out. He told Darlene that one night in bed and she started to cry.

"Christ, Klaus, get out of there. You're killing your-self."

That was the night Klaus told her about the summer he worked with his father. He'd never told anyone about that, not even Epp. A week after finishing Grade 11, Klaus took the bus to Calgary. His father met him at the station. They hadn't seen each other in eight years, and Klaus was embarrassed to discover his dad was balding, and stank so pungently of hot brine that Klaus's eyes burned. When they shook hands, Klaus felt the frailness of his own fingers in the old man's grip. They drove straight to the shop, The Baker Mann.

"You remember the shop, Klaus?"

Klaus nodded. He used to have a nightmare about being trapped in it.

When they arrived his father unlocked the double deadbolts, pushed open the steel-framed door, then said he'd give Klaus a tour.

"This is the oven, this is the slicer, these are the mixers. I got two good mixers, but I tell you something." He held up his hands. "These are better. Over here is the flour: rye, whole wheat, bleached. Careful, that's a rat trap. They come over from Pederman's. I am taking him to court. Damages. My customers see one of Pederman's rats over here then what? City tries shutting me down. I kill the bugger that happens."

Klaus looked at the handsaws on the wall. Eight of them. Two rows of four. Each blade clumsily painted with a snow scene of chalets, sledding children, and Christmas trees. His father's hobby, from the old days when he had time for such things.

"Out front here is where we serve the customers. Remember? Juice, sausage rolls, coffee, tea, everything they want but no free refills. Remember that. I got only one rule: no free refills." His father faced him. "So Klaus, you are seventeen. Your mother says you never work before."

"I picked blueberries."

"When I am fourteen years I was full-time working. That was thirty-two years ago. You got a girl?"

"No."

"When I am fifteen years I'm banging three beavers every night. Your hair's too long. I can't have hair in my dough. Customers see hair in my dough what they will think? I only got one rule: no hair in the dough." He searched a drawer beneath the work bench. "Here."

Klaus frowned at the packet of nylons.

"On your head."

Klaus peeled open the cellophane and drew out the tan nylons.

"Come on, come on, ten minutes we are opening."

Klaus pulled one over his head and tucked his hair up inside. The rest of the nylon dangled like a nightcap down his back.

His father thrust a broom at him. "Start from scratch. You learn the business from the bottom up. Not too proud to sweep a floor, are you?"

"No."

"Good."

His father yanked open the door of the walk-in fridge, rolled out a tub of dough, hoisted an armful onto the slab-wood bench and set to work beating it like a boxer working out on the heavy bag.

By noon, Klaus was beating dough right alongside him. By one, his hands had seized shut with cramps.

"Give me your hand. I fix your cramp." His father forced the fingers open making Klaus shout. "There you go. Any more problems you tape an aspirin to it. You get over cramps real fast around here. Cramps mean one thing: weak hands. I got no use for weak hands. You got to have strong hands, Klaus, strong hands. It's the only way. Otherwise you never survive."

The Baker Mann stayed open until six. They broke for supper: kaiser rolls, sliced cheese, ham, strudel, and beer. Klaus's father drank Becks.

"Only beer in the world. Remember that. The rest you can wash your car with it."

They sat at one of the tables and watched the street. His father leaned hard on his elbows, slapping flaps of ham into his mouth, then chewing disdainfully. "There the bastard he is now."

They watched Pederman, who owned the Schnitzel Haus next door, get into a black BMW driven by a young man.

"He's a queer, Pederman. You know what is a queer, Klaus?"

Klaus nodded, embarrassed.

"You watch. Soon they run him out of town. Calgary

they don't like queers. Send him to Vancouver. Full of queers, Vancouver. So you are doing like shit in school. Your mother said you fail chemistry. I teach you chemistry. Yeast. That is chemistry. Bread and beer, Klaus. In both of them, yeast is number one ingredient. In the old days, the baker and brewer are the same. There. I teach you some history too."

They worked all evening mixing dough, rolling it out for pastry, then pouring in the filling while the bread rose in the proofbox. His father's scalp seeped sweat that ran down his skull to the end of his nose where it dangled before dropping into the dough.

"I only got one rule, Klaus: no slack-assing off. You want to slack-ass off, you can leave. Pederman he is a slack-ass. One more year he is out of business. Guaranteed. And you know why he is a slack-ass? Because he is a drunk. A drunk and a queer."

They worked on amid the wet and hanging fug of the raw dough bloating quietly in the heat. His father worked in a silent fury, beating the dough, flipping it, folding it, beating it more. "She has a boyfriend?"

Klaus was silent.

"Don't lie, Klaus. I got only one rule: never lie to me."

"Sometimes."

He kept hitting the dough with his fists. From ten to eleven they cleaned up. At eleven Kurt Mann slapped the flour from his hands, took a bottle of schnapps from the freezer and poured them each a shot. "Okay, Klaus. Bedtime. Here. I buy this for you." He gave him an air mattress and a pump. Then his father cleared the empty flour sacks and plastic pails from an army cot, and, boots still on his feet, lay down in his dough-scabbed whites. On the wall above him hung the saw-blades. "Tomorrow we do some real work."

Klaus just stood there holding the air mattress and pump. "What happened to the house?"

"House? What the hell I am needing a house for?" He gulped loudly from the bottle of schnapps. "No. Better I live here. Protect my investment. See this?" He reached under the cot and held up a crowbar. "At night is when Pederman his rats come. I told Pederman I kill him and he threatened to take me to court. I said fine, take me to court. I explain the judge everything and you will be out of business like that. Already he has bribed the health inspectors. I don't need to bribe health inspectors. They come here I show them everything. You just go there and look at that wall. Go on, Klaus look at that wall. There. No, there. Ya. That's a permit. Passed. No problem. I got only one rule: no problems. That's why I don't like Pederman. I'm going to tell you something Klaus, are you listening? Your mother ran away. That's abandoning. I don't like abandoning. Everyone is abandoning these days. I got only one rule:

no abandoning. I never abandon nothing in my life. I stay. I stick it out. I finish what I start."

When Klaus finished the story, Darlene said, "You're not him, Klaus. You're nothing like that."

"He wasn't either until he opened that shop."

That caught her by surprise.

He could see Darlene's silhouette beside him in bed. It was summer, the window open, and the branches of the apple tree in the backyard shuffled against each other in a faint wind. Klaus didn't know how to explain it, other than by describing the time he and his father stole apples together.

"How old were you?"

"Six."

"You're kidding."

"Got caught, too." Klaus felt himself smiling as he remembered old man Wodinski and his fruit trees. "We planned it all out: get up at dawn, sneak over and do it. It was his idea."

Darlene still didn't believe it. "Your father's?"

"Yeah. He was going to make all these apple pies, right. Because these were cooking apples. And Wodinski never used them. Just let them fall and rot. Had a whole orchard. So anyway, we're up in the tree and my old man he lets this fart."

"No way."

"A big blaster. And we both start laughing. And so

then I fart. And then he does another one. Pretty soon we're sticking apples in our mouths to keep from laughing. But there's no way. It's too late. The porch door whacks open and Wodinski comes running out. Not only is he carrying an axe, he starts chopping the tree while we're in it. So my dad starts chucking apples to drive him back. We go running up the alley with Wodinski behind us, but he was barefoot so couldn't run on the gravel. He calmed down when my dad gave him a couple of pies. Only time I ever saw my dad really laugh, I mean really let go. In those days he worked in a mass-production place like Bestbuy."

"Yeah?"

Klaus nodded. "We had a field trip there in Grade One."

"To the bakery?"

"The whole class. And he led the tour."

"Your dad?"

"Yup. Was like Disneyland. Five of us got our picture taken inside a mixer. It was that big. Could mix a dough the size of a couch. There was tons of everything. Bins of raisins, sunflower seeds, sesame seeds, poppy seeds, flax seeds. And all these old Germans with forearms like Popeye. It smelled good, too. That was the thing, it smelled good. They made things you could eat. We all got cinnamon buns at the end of the tour."

"And it was your dad."

83

"Uh huh." Klaus lay there in the dark, remembering. "The next year he opened his own bakery. We never stole apples again."

§

Wong walked in at nine and found Graves and Singh waiting. "What?"

"Had a bit of trouble last night," said Singh.

When Singh got to the part about Epp jumping in the river, Wong felt the cement floor tilt like the deck of a destroyer in a steep sea. He patted his coat for his codeines. "Why wasn't I called?"

"It was four in the morning."

"Show me."

Singh led the way. They passed Klaus loading the oven, Mutton working the proof box, Bell on pans, and Stahl overseeing the divider. When the procession had passed, every one of them turned to watch.

Wong inspected Epp's barricade of blue plastic bread trays, then stood with his hands behind his back and stared at the forklift that lay like a toppled tank. The scratch on his left lens continued to distract him, an ongoing reminder that he'd been assaulted. Of course, they'd closed ranks. It was to be expected. But such insubordination could not pass unpunished.

"And he's gone."

"Jumped in the river."

Wong walked away.

Graves and Singh looked at each other, then hurried to catch up.

As Wong crossed the bakery he felt the eyes of the men on him, so he flexed his jaw muscles, frowned, and stared straight ahead: the general deep in deliberation. He wanted to ask more questions, but he'd wait. First, he'd make Singh think it was his fault. Wong knew Singh was a solid supervisor, but no man was above a carefully administered dose of disapproval. Self-doubt would make young Singh work harder. Self-doubt would keep him in line. As Wong expected, Singh and Graves caught up with him at the stairs leading to his office. Wong turned at the fifth step, ensuring an intimidating height advantage from which to lecture.

"Those men make twenty—" He caught himself. "Fifteen dollars an hour. They get five weeks holiday, plus their birthday's off with pay. Yet if the newspapers get hold of this they'll make Bestbuy look like a salt mine. Remember what happened with that fingernail-in-the-dough business." He stared down at them like Napoleon from his horse until their guilty gazes dropped. "If Back East hears they might just say, Hell, forget the wage cut—shut the place down." Wong employed a dramatic pause to let this point press like a gun barrel to their heads. "Report to my office in one hour."

Now Wong sat rubbing the gunshot wound in the centre of his right palm, thinking about the hatred in their eyes last night. To the men it was his fault, he was the company, he was Back East. He'd felt them struggle to hold themselves in check as he'd walked out. He'd smelled their anger in the raw-onion stink of their sweat. They hated him. They hated him for his authority and they hated him because he was Chinese. He continued rubbing the scar on his hand. His wife Mercedes insisted it looked like the stigmata. Wong thought it looked like what it was, a bullet wound. He slid open the bottom right drawer, took out his binoculars, and stepped to the window. The general manager's office commanded a view of the entire plant. Given the conveyors, the haze of flour dust, and the angle of the lights, Wong knew the men could see only his silhouette. He'd considered installing a two-way mirror, but one Saturday evening he'd made Mercedes stand up there while he stood down below on the floor, and he discovered he preferred the effect of the silhouette: imposing, dark, an *eminence grise* as the French would say, and C.P. Wong knew that was good. Keep them at a distance. Keep them in awe. Fear—the great motivator. He'd learned this early, from watching his grandmother bully his father, who was simultaneously manipulated by his wife, Wong's mother, who now bullied him, while Mercedes, awaiting her own ascendancy, operated from the wings.

Mercedes came from Honduras. Wong had been born in Vancouver. Mercedes's photo had been mailed to him by a matchmaker in Hong Kong who had contacts with Chinese communities all over the world.

So, standing at the window, Wong made the most of his silhouette. He inflated his chest and stood very still. No squirrelly twitching, no tics and habits to mock or mimic. Let them discover him up here—the general in all his terrible grandeur.

What Wong really wanted was to have entered the Canadian Army. As a boy, he'd enjoyed many idyllic afternoons melting the heads off his plastic soldiers. He'd soak model ships in oil, then set them ablaze and launch them down the back alley ditch imagining Drake's fire-ships routing the Armada. But Wong's military career was thwarted by his eyes; he was legally blind without his combination of contact lenses and glasses. Still, he monitored world events. He had a subscription to *Jane's Defence Weekly*. He staged mock battles, deploying his forces on a computer screen, waging war with African warlords crazed on diets of monkey meat and ganja.

Wong had been lucky last year when he shot himself in the hand. The bullet passed between the bones, piercing the flesh joining the thumb and forefinger. It didn't even bleed at first, as if his hand was as shocked as his eyes. There was a hot sting followed by the smell of

singed pork, and then a strange heat began boiling its
way up his arm. He'd been admiring the Mauser, weigh-
ing it in the palm of his hand, holding it at arm's length,
and BANG! His hit hand leapt as if jerked by a wire.
He'd looked from the pistol to the hole punched in his
palm to the pistol again. He'd laid the Mauser on his
desk, listened, reminded himself that Enfield and
Wesson were at Chinese class and Mercedes at the bou-
tique, then watched the blood appear, like a cinema trick,
filling that hole in his hand and running down his wrist
in the manner of those grisly Christ statues he'd seen in
Honduras when he'd flown down to meet Mercedes.
Wong knew more than enough about ordnance to
understand that he owed the neatness of the hole to the
Mauser's slim 7.65 millimetre bore and the bullet's full
metal jacket.

To save the Bokhara from blood, he'd crossed to the
bathroom and leaned nauseated over the sink. Yet the
thought of that ten-dollar-per-pound salmon steak
being barfed down the bowl made him hold on. He ran
cold water and splashed his face. He washed his palm
numb, but the pain resurfaced at his elbow, more intense,
beating his bicep with a lead pipe. He struggled with the
childproof cap of the codeines and dry-swallowed five,
wrapped his hand in gauze with the help of his teeth and
wondered if he looked sexy leaning there like a wound-
ed Rambo. Reeling off yards of toilet paper, he wiped

the sink and counter and floor. Then he returned to his
study. The bullet had passed through his hand and hit
their wedding picture. Oh God. A hole right through
Mercedes's belly, the glass webbed but still intact, and
Mercedes with a gunshot in the gut. Wong knew his
wife was superstitious enough to take this as a sign, an
omen, proof of Wong's subconscious animosity, of the
fact that he thought she was cheap, and suspected he'd
been deceived into a bad match. She'd go to the doctor,
she'd start waking at night with abdominal pains, she'd
ask why the bullet hit her and not him, she'd visit that
psychic and ask about the evil eye. Worst of all, she'd
know he had a gun, and she'd seen enough of those in
Honduras, where one hundred U.S. dollars bought you
an AK 47, and just about anything else you wanted,
from grenades to flame throwers, all of it left over from
the wars in Nicaragua and El Salvador. Wong still suspected that that was all he was to her, a plane ticket out
of Central America. Hadn't she begun avoiding him in
bed as soon as he got her into the country? She'd stay
up late until he was asleep, or she turned in early and
had her earplugs in and eye-mask on when he got under
the covers.

When Wong took down the shattered wedding picture, he discovered that the bullet had punched a hole
through the Laura Ashley wallpaper behind it. He went
into the master bedroom and saw where the bullet had

emerged and, because of the trajectory, hit the ceiling, gouging a ragged groove a foot long as it entered right above the bed. Checking his watch, he saw the blue-black bruise spreading from under the bloody gauze on his hand. Eight forty-five. He had to pick up the kids in fifteen minutes. He thought how dangerous Vancouver had become; your kids couldn't walk two blocks on their own for fear of perverts.

§

By ten in the morning Singh had been on shift twelve hours. He'd passed through the various phases of fatigue that ranged from dull drowsiness to weepy exhaustion. He sat in his office, directly below Wong's, and waited for Graves, who finally emerged from the toilet struggling with the buttons on his pants. Graves had topped all the fingers on his right hand running the slicers back when he was still in the union. He'd felt no more pain than a candleflame across the knuckles. One instant he had fingernails and the next—ZING!—stubs.

Joining Singh, Graves said, "I don't like this."

"Me neither."

Graves looked around. "You ever wonder why they call it a lavatory?"

"The can?"

"Yeah."

"Lavatory," said Singh, recalling his Latin, "from *lavatorium*, from *lavare*, to wash."

Graves stared. "The old lady's got a bar of lava soap."

"Uh huh."

"Takes three baths a day that woman."

"Is that right."

"Tub's always full of hair."

Singh watched Graves. He knew that Graves, as a devout Presbyterian, must view him as a godless pagan destined for the flames of hell. "Well?"

Graves looked at his watch. "Fifty-eight minutes."

They lingered. Wong had said an hour, and as he'd explained the one and only time they'd arrived early for a meeting, an hour had sixty minutes, not fifty-eight, not sixty-two, but sixty. They looked down the length of the shipping dock at the stacked rows of blue plastic bread trays. A dying fluorescent tube twitched. Singh knew Wong would blame him. Wong had made one thing clear when he promoted Singh:

"The first rule of management is this: Shit doesn't just happen. Not here at Bestbuy."

The interview had taken place upstairs in Wong's office. It was the first time they'd talked, the first time Singh had been upstairs, and the first time he learned that each Bestbuy employee had a file. His lay open on Wong's blotter. Wong had asked what Singh was doing in a mass-production bakery with a poli-sci degree.

"This place got me that degree."

"Do you like it here?"

Singh had expected that question. In the days leading up to the interview, he'd devised responses to all the questions Wong might reasonably ask. "I find satisfaction in efficiency."

Wong hadn't looked impressed by such an obviously rehearsed response. "Where do you see yourself in five years?"

"Here."

"And if I don't offer you a supervisor position?"

That had caught Singh. What did Wong want to hear? That Singh was a loyal employee who'd stick with the team? Or that Singh sought the challenges of career satisfaction? He got bold. "Somewhere else."

Wong nodded.

Singh saw champagne.

But Wong was not finished. "The transition from union to management comes down to one thing: responsibility. You'll have to care. Because only those who care take responsibility. And only those who take responsibility are fit to supervise." Wong went to the window and gazed out over the factory floor. "You realize you'll lose friends. All those guys down there, all your union brothers, they'll resent you." Wong faced him. "You'll have to get mad at them. When one slacks off, you'll have to confront him. Even if you used to be buddies, you'll have to put his nose in his own dirt. You. Because you're responsible. And I'll be on your back if you're not on theirs. It's important you know this. It's important you understand that work will no longer be a matter of drifting in and wandering around. It will be a matter of taking charge, of knowing what is going on, of talking to your foremen, of consulting with the engineers, of taking responsibility for everything that happens out there. Everything." Wong had watched for Singh's reaction and Singh nodded, meaning, Yes, sir. "So. Think it over. Take a week."

Singh had left Wong's office inspired and terrified. He'd driven home to Richmond oblivious to the traffic. At the time, Singh still lived with his parents, fending off their attempts to find him a good Sikh girl from a good Sikh family. When he got home that evening he said nothing of the job offer. It was his decision, not theirs, a point of view that in itself would cause a crisis in the clan and set his mother to wailing and cracking her knuckles. He went for a walk after supper. He walked a long time, unable to decide, until, on the way back he wandered into the 7-Eleven to pick up a *Sports Illustrated*. He saw the elderly Indian behind the counter in his 7-Eleven smock selling Scratch & Wins and Slurpees, a man Singh knew held a degree from an Indian university. He decided right there to take responsibility.

"Fifty-nine-and-a-half."

They slowly climbed the stairs.

Glenda and Gail, the twin sisters who worked payroll, eyed Singh and Graves over top of their glasses. Gail had a poodle engraved in the corner of her right lens, Glenda a sickle moon and star. Glenda cast horoscopes. She and Gail had been on community TV demonstrating their ability to read each other's minds. The twins were fifty, had both buried two husbands, and both favoured black and grey to complement their red hair. Wong's wife knew them because each month she went for tarot and palm readings, and aura analysis. Wong, the same age as Glenda and Gail, thought it was all a lot of bunk, but he also thought they looked pretty good, and when his mind was not occupied by bakery business or the finer points of military strategy, he dwelled on his lack of a sex life, which led to fantasies of a *menage a trois* right here in the office with the buxom twins.

Graves strode on past Glenda and Gail shutting his mind to protect himself from their necromancy. He kept his eyes down because their red hair made him think of red pubic hair, which made him think of devils copulating in the sulphurous boudoirs of hell. Graves took an active role in the church. He'd beaten the bottle after thirty years of sullen silent drinking, and nightmares of bat-faced babies. The time he set fire to the bed, which burned blue with the alcohol in the sweat-soaked sheets, had illuminated his way to the Lord.

Singh gave the ladies a peace sign.

Glenda, the more mischievous, winked and smiled and willed Singh an erection. It was a little trick she'd been working on. An exercise in creative visualization.

When they entered the office, Wong gestured them to chairs. Wong glittered: gold watch, ring, cufflinks, tie pin, glasses. Singh's gaze skipped from glint to glint, ending at Wong's face.

"Who called Keegan?"

Singh and Graves glanced at each other.

"He's on his way now. And after last night he's out for blood. If this Epp drowns we're dead. The papers will find out, which means Toronto will find out, which means New York will find out. The Americans are the ones who make the real decisions. And they're looking for any excuse they can to shut the place down."

Wong always invoked the spectre of Back East when he wanted to frighten them. And it worked. Back East created visions of men in suits, men from Toronto, or worse: the U.S., cold men with digital eyes; men who knew things.

Graves looked at the floor.

Singh crossed his legs to hide his hard-on.

Wong let them consider the consequences. Then, when he judged the time right, he became fatherly. "Hell, Pat, what the heck happened?"

Singh narrated the night all over again.

95

Wong raised a forefinger. "What was the key doing in the forklift?"

"The key's always in the forklift."

"Do you know how much that forklift cost?"

Singh stared at Wong's nameplate: CP WONG. No, he didn't.

"Twenty-eight thousand dollars. It's three months old. They have accountants Back East who want us to recycle bread crumbs. How do you think they're going to react when they see I've purchased another forkift?"

"You're hardly going to need a new one."

Wong raised his hand silencing Graves.

Singh hunched forward trying to appear deeply troubled. He'd passed beyond fatigue to indifference. And his hard-on reminded him that he had a life beyond the bakery, a pregnant wife, and a daughter on the way. Though if he got canned over this they'd be living in a basement suite, or worse, with one of his cousins.

Wong opened the folder on his desk. "Epp, Martin Ronald." Wong shrugged inside the silk shell of his suit. "Who is he? I've never seen him. Three years and I've never seen his face. Who is this Epp?" Wong frowned. His eyebrows were not eyebrows, but two rows of widely spaced hairs. Singh thought he could probably count the number of hairs and it would be no more than a dozen in each one. Singh's eyebrows met to form one solid hedge.

"He works nights."

"It says he's been employed here going on twenty-two years. Yet he's still on nights?"

"He's accident prone."

Wong read back through the First Aid reports. He found the letters Klaus had written under Epp's name requesting transfer onto days. Wong eyed both Singh and Graves. He tapped the papers. "Keegan's got copies. He'll take this to Labour Relations. Going to bat for this Epp will be his way to get in good again with the men." Wong stood now and went to the window and spoke with his back to them. "If Epp drowns we'll end up in court. That fingernail business will be nothing." Wong referred to the nail clippings discovered in the Hovis two summers ago. He stood with his hands behind him. Graves, meanwhile, slipped a finger onto his pulse and eyed his Timex. Wong let the silence spread like a stain. He'd studied silence. He knew what it could accomplish and how best to employ it. No, this wasn't fingernail clippings in the Hovis—and he recalled how far out of hand that had got. Some customer had written a letter to the editor, which sparked other letters about objects found in Bestbuy bread, hairs, feathers, a condom. A freelancer showed up wanting to tour the plant. Back East heard. He got a fax: What was going on out there? They'd hired him to turn the Vancouver plant around. What was all this about fingernails in the Hovis?

"Let me tell you something," said Wong. "There's a man in town right now from Back East who'd rather this place shut its doors today. If he finds out about Epp we might as well jump in the river, too."

Graves, with only two years to retirement, settled into a relaxed attitude and drawled. "Oh, I think we'll see Young Epp Monday night as per usual."

Wong directed his formidable focus upon Graves, implying he'd hold him to that. Graves appeared all too at ease for Wong's taste.

"You're the Head Supervisor. I hold you responsible."

Graves reacted like he'd been slapped. "Now wait a minute. I wasn't even there."

"You knew about the letters."

Graves clapped his dentured mouth shut. He and Singh had both read them aloud, hooting over Epp's prose style: 'Inasmuch as I embody 20 years of senyerority it is inkumbent upon myself, and you, in full conshence, to stand upon my rightful rights as a rightful member in real good and law abiding standing of the International Bruthcrhood of the Bakery Werkers Union . . . '

"You knew about the letters and did nothing."

"Well what would you have done?" Anger edged his voice. Graves had thirteen years on Wong and yet Wong was his boss. Graves had worked forty-four years in the bakeries and they went and made Wong GM over him.

"Talk to him. Sit him down and talk to him. Did you do that? Either of you?"

"I talk to him every night," said Singh.

"And?"

"I wouldn't trust him to wash my car." And then, hoping to divert blame, added, "I'd like to know who hired him in the first place."

Wong saw Singh's ploy and also saw a way of using it; he turned and gave Graves the skeptical eye.

"Don't you look at me. You know damn well that's Keegan's end."

Now that Graves was acceptably anxious, Wong again deployed silence, letting them listen to the brassy blare of the factory below and dwell on the consequences of their irresponsibility. Then he demonstrated why he was Wong: the Man, the general manager. "All right. Good. You're on the right track. The man's a millstone. What I see is this—Epp is a hazard. His record proves it. All things considered, Bestbuy has acted like a charity employing a man with a grade eight education and paying him twenty dollars an hour. Now, I've been rereading the seniority clause." Wong fought the urge to smile in pride at the loophole he'd discovered, and once again thought he should have gone into corporate law. He raised his forefinger and quoted: 'Seniority earns an employee access to the job site. Seniority, however, does not give said employee any say

99

in what job function he or she actually performs. That is left to the discretion of management.' Wong eyed them through the scrape on his lens. "That's you. With Epp's record we have every right to keep him pushing a broom. And our friend Keegan should know that."

"Exactly," said Graves, as if Wong was merely rephrasing his own words.

Singh, however, was not as impressed. "Maybe in theory, but not in practice. Jobs here always go by seniority. Always." He looked at Graves. "You know that."

Graves looked at Wong. "Exactly."

"The fact remains—"

"—This shop has always honoured seniority," said Singh. "And anyway, that clause misses the point, which is the shift, not the job. Epp wanted off graveyard, not off janitor work. That's what a lawyer will argue."

Wong didn't like Singh cutting him off, but Singh had a point and Wong was too smart to ignore it.

Graves watched Singh and Wong and realized he was missing the point. "Don't the company have an attorney?"

Wong became impatient. "Yes, the company has many attorneys. But we don't want Back East to know, do we. We can't have this get out of hand. Even if we went to court and won we'd lose, because it's bad PR, and Back East doesn't like bad PR. So this has to be kept quiet. This has to be sorted out immediately." He checked his watch. "Keegan'll be here any minute. Stall him. Tell him I'm not available."

When Graves and Singh were gone, Wong looked at the beige telephone on his desk. It occured to him that he hated beige. It was vague. He liked red. He picked up the receiver and punched 9.

"Gail. Get me the Airport Inn, will you please." Anxiety burned his stomach like a gulp of boiling vinegar. As Wong waited, he stared through the scratch on his lens at the scar on his palm and realized that, far from the stigmata, it looked like a tiny asshole. He had an asshole in the palm of his hand. The phone started ringing, diverting him from the profundity of this realization. He drew himself up straight. The hotel operator said hello. Wong said, "Kyle Hunt, please." There came another ring then someone picked up.

"Hello?"

"It's Wong."

"Wongo! How'd it go?"

"They accepted it."

"Told you. Wongo, hold on a minute." Hunt's voice became muffled as he spoke to someone in the room.

As Wong waited, he recalled their meeting last week in the lounge of the Airport Inn. It had taken place immediately before Wong had met Keegan at The Blue Boy.

The lounge of the Airport Inn had chrome-and-

leather chairs, a black carpet patterned with gold airplanes, and raku bowls of miniature Japanese crackers
on each of the smoked glass tables. Hunt, young and
silk-suited, had flown out First Class from Canada
Bestbuy's head office Back East. He got straight to the
point.

"It's cut back or close down."

"Five-twenty-five an hour?"

"It's the only way."

"You're suggesting a twenty-five percent pay cut."

"Stating, not suggesting."

"They'll strike."

"We'll padlock the doors."

"Just like that?"

"Yup." Hunt downed the last of his martini. Then he
relented a little. "Wongo. The Vancouver plant's been
running at a loss."

"We've bounced back eight percent since I started."

"Hey. You gave the place legs again. Everyone's seriously impressed. But it's still losing." Hunt scanned the
lounge for the waitress. "Where is she?"

"Seems to me what Back East really wants is to shut
down and move south," said Wong.

Hunt didn't deny it. "And they want you to go south
too."

"Seattle?" Wong was horrified.

"Why not? Vancouver's a milltown."

There was so much bread being shipped north each night from Seattle that the Vancouver plant's production had dropped to half. Wong looked out the window. The tinted glass gave the corrugated cloud cover a strangely greenish hue, as if the clouds were feeling nauseous. Wong sipped his martini even though he hated martinis. Hunt had ordered them.

Now Hunt dug into the glazed clay bowl for the last of the Japanese crackers. "How's the food here? Can you get wild salmon?"

Wong knew Hunt from Back East. Six years ago they'd been paired up in the annual Bestbuy Golf Tourney. Hunt ran a handicap of five; Wong lost five balls on the first hole. A year later Wong had gone to the Hamilton plant, then Winnipeg, and then out to Calgary before ending up back on the coast.

"I want sockeye," said Hunt. "Wild sockeye."

Hunt's cheeks made Wong think of toad bellies, pale and smooth except for a line that ran from his left nostril to the corner of his mouth. A sneer line. It made Wong think of a dueling scar. Except duels implied honour.

Hunt scanned the lounge for Sushila, the waitress. When ordering the martinis he'd made a point of reading her name clip aloud and complimenting her on how sweet it sounded. Wong had watched hoping the girl would whack Hunt with her metal tray. She didn't.

"Keegan'll flip," said Wong.

"There she is." Hunt raised his forefinger as if making a bid in a silent auction. "How about Alaskan King Crab?"

Wong considered crab nothing more than glorified spider. "I don't eat shellfish. Keegan'll demand to see the books."

"So show him."

"He'll say they're doctored."

"He can say whatever he wants. The contract's up and this is the offer. It's free trade. It's the Americans. They want those jobs for Seattle." Hunt watched Sushila make her way past the black leather chairs. "How old do you think she is?"

It took Wong a moment before he realized Hunt meant Sushila. "Twenty."

"I wonder if she likes sex."

Wong thought of Mercedes. She was thirty-six, fourteen years younger than him. She used to like sex. "How's Jane?"

"Pregnant."

Wong followed Hunt's gaze as it traced Sushila's movements. "Congratulations. When's she due?"

Hunt continued eyeing Sushila. "October. No. January."

Wong checked his watch. In an hour he had to meet Keegan and present Bestbuy's offer. The thought made his headache pound harder. His codeines were out in the car.

"This'll be my fourth move in six years. You know what this is doing to my kids?" Yet Wong saw that Hunt considered the issue closed.

"If they go for the cut-back then you could be here who knows, another year."

"That's it?"

"Maybe two. Depends." Hunt's scalp showed through his remaining hair and his blue suit shone like sheet metal. "You'll like Seattle."

"Sure. Three times the murder rate."

"Wongo. American dollars."

But Wong's head hurt too much to think of American dollars. Rubbing his temples he saw the gunshot scar. Mercedes had almost left him over it.

The waitress reached their table.

"Ah, Su-shila." Hunt clapped his hands then rubbed them together as if he had mucho big plans for her.

She said nothing, just observed him coolly with her blunt black eyes.

§

Hunt came back to the phone. "Wongo. Sorry. So. They voted to accept the cut."

"And almost killed me."

"Management's not a popularity contest. Look, I need to drop by and take some snaps."

"Snaps?"

"Photographs."

"Where?"

"There. For Back East. Accounting wants specs on the layout and the machinery."

"Here?"

"Yeah. So comb your hair."

"Today?"

"Every day. Hundred strokes. Your hair will love you for it."

When Hunt hung up Wong put the phone down and tried to think. Hunt would see the forklift out back. He'd ask questions. He'd take pictures. He'd find out about Epp.

§

"What the bloody hell happened here last night?" said Keegan. He, Graves, and Singh were seated in the lunchroom. "Got a union brother jumping in the river and another in the hospital. I was just on the horn to Donnelly. Poor bugger needs a bone specialist and jigsaw champion to put his foot back together."

"Now Hank—"

"Now Hank nothin'. Epp's been on my ass a year now because you people won't deal. I got more complaints re this shop than all the others combined. Forty-five years I've been in the bakeries. Forty-five years. That's longer'n you been on this green earth, Singh. And you, Graves, and Wong are the problem." Keegan stopped for a breath, sipped at his coffee, and grimaced as if he was drinking soap. "Is this canned milk? Why don't you get some two-percent and a juice machine? Spring for a bucket of paint while you're at it and brighten this place up. Maybe your men won't look like they just drew life without parole at goddamn Kent. As Union President I intend to lay charges on behalf of Martin Epp for malicious and unfair treatment. Twenty-two years seniority. Man has twenty-two years seniority and he's still dumping flour. Now what the hell kind of nonsense is that? I'll tell you what kind. It's a conspiracy is what it is. A goddamn management con-spiracy. And Singh, you and Wong and Graves are all in on it. Now, I don't have to tell you how long it takes a man to build up twenty-two years seniority. I've got copies of the letters. He's got a grievance. I've tried arranging a meeting but you guys won't play ball and I know why. This is just one more act of noncooperation in Wong's plan to break our local. Well, over my ass. You put us up against the wall last night. But there's still something called law and order. I'm meeting with Camponi this afternoon and believe you me someone's gonna be doing time for criminal negligence. Now, where's Wong?"

"Come on, Hank." Graves knew Hank Keegan from the fifties when they'd both jobbed in the old Weston's. "Don't you think you're a little fast out of the blocks here? Epp'll show as usual, grinning like a monkey."

But Keegan declined the buddy-buddy. He'd never liked Stab-in-the-back Graves and the paths they'd chosen proved their differences—Keegan went union and Graves went management. And Keegan liked him even less since Graves had become a Holy Roller.

Keegan took a drag off his cigarette. "I'll tell you what I think. I think I've been too slow out of the damn blocks is what I think. What about Epp's grievance? I walk in here and what do I see but college kids on day shift and a twenty-year man on graveyard?"

Graves inclined his head as if to say: you can do better than that. "That's temporary and you know it. Those kids'll be on graveyard bun production starting the week after next and they'll stay there all summer."

Keegan took a shot off his inhaler. "Buns my blue ass. Epp's got twenty-two years seniority. Now where's Wong?"

Graves continued smiling. He glanced at Singh and invited him to admire Keegan's Irish obstinance. Then he played his ace. "The facts are these and you should know them: seniority gets a man into the plant, but does in no way give him any say over what function he performs."

"I'd like to perform a function on you. You think you're God Almighty with your nose up management's arse, don't you. Well don't forget this: when the time comes they'll crap you into a hole. Now where's Wong?"

"He'll talk to you when the facts are in, not before."

"Fine. Wong won't talk to me, he can talk to the police."

"When?"

Keegan looked at Singh. "Soon as they're here is when."

"No. When did you ever try arranging a meeting to discuss Epp's complaint?"

Keegan saw where Singh was going. "Lotsa times."

Singh looked to Graves. "I don't recall any requests for a meeting about Epp."

"Exactly."

"Then you got a bad memory." Keegan got up and poured himself another coffee. Epp's letters were so messed up Keegan couldn't make out half of what they said. Anyway, he'd had more important problems, like his son Jimmy in prison, like his wife flinging money around in Reno, like his own future, like the union's future. Who the hell was Epp when Keegan had the good of the entire local to think of? Okay, he should've been Johnny-on-the-spot and gone to bat for the bugger. But that phone rang with complaints all goddamn day.

No one seemed to realize that the great days of the sixties and seventies were finished. Back then they could bend management over the bargaining table and put it to them. Now it was the other way around, and he was getting blamed. Well who was to blame for Epp?

Stirring his coffee with his back to Graves and Singh, Keegan got an idea. A lawsuit. Against the company. On behalf of Epp. It would redeem him with the membership. He'd call the papers, he'd call the radio, he'd call the TV, he'd hand out leaflets downtown if he had to. He couldn't afford to get voted out of the office now. Not at his age. He turned from the coffee machine and pointed with a spoon. "You buggers killed him. You buggers're gonna pay."

CHAPTER FIVE

The Funeral Procession

THE CITY POLICE FINALLY ARRIVED as Singh was heading out the door. They turned him around and walked him back in. Eleven in the morning, five hours after Singh had called them. Kyle Hunt, his timing infallible, arrived right behind the cops. All four marched up to Wong's office. At the sight of Hunt, Wong's face went as white as a block of lard. Hunt, however, was smiling. He was also carrying a Nikon. The Vancouver plant was proving entertaining. Best of all, the place was shooting itself in the foot and practically begging to be shut down. Back East would be pleased.

"Wongo."

Soon Keegan and Graves joined the crowd.

Wong led them down the stairs and onto the factory floor as if leading his own funeral procession.

When Klaus saw the cops, his first thought was that they were coming to arrest him for arson. Would he be able to plead temporary insanity because he'd been drunk? Then he thought: no, they found Epp's body. He corrected himself: Epp's corpse. He pried the sponge plug from his ear, and the bakery soundtrack jumped close.

Klaus said, "Did you find him?"

Singh shook his head.

Klaus's pulse dropped.

The younger cop, new to the job, glanced around as if watching the conveyors and vents for snipers. The older cop had a massive head that suggested a bone structure of stone. His receding hair had left an island-like tuft up front, which was matched in its reddish colour by a well-scrubbed moustache. He had a pen and a pad, and his gut sagged doughishly over his belt just like Klaus's. The cop's name was McNeil, and he was wondering what he always wondered in these food production plants, which was whether or not the workers, knowing what they did, bought their own product. What he said, however, was, "I understand you were Mr. Epp's friend."

The word "friend" smacked Klaus like a bread pan across the skull. He endured a moment of panic, certain that Epp's pleading voice would hound him to the grave, that he'd sit up in bed at night hearing Epp, that when he closed his eyes, he'd see Epp floating down river. Epp, who feared water and couldn't swim. And once again he recalled writing those letters. At first Epp had wanted to be there when Klaus wrote them, to be sure Klaus got it right. But Klaus said no way, he couldn't write like that. He mentioned those signs mechanics often have in their shops:

HOURLY RATE: $20

IF CUSTOMER WATCHES: $30

Epp reluctantly agreed, but still wanted to see the letters. He also wanted to deliver them personally. Klaus said bad idea. The letters would carry more weight if they arrived in the mail. It was more official. Yet there was nothing Klaus could say to avoid letting Epp see the letters beforehand. So Klaus, despising himself, watched in horror as he wrote two letters each time, one a cogently argued plea on Epp's behalf, and the second a burlesque of the first. The second was the one that got put into the envelope. Klaus also advised Epp against badgering Keegan or Singh. When Epp said that the squeaky wheel got the grease, Klaus said this wasn't cars but people.

"Yes, I was his friend."

"Was he acting strangely?"

"No."

"Depressed?"

"No more than usual."

"So he was usually depressed."

Klaus saw Singh and Graves to the right of the cop and Keegan, Hunt and Wong to the left. "He wanted off graveyard and they wouldn't let him."

"Who?"

Klaus hesitated only a moment, his eyes cutting from Wong to Keegan and back to Wong again. "Management."

The cop nodded and wrote, then Wong led the funeral procession out back where Singh described the events all over again.

Klaus, meanwhile, resumed loading the oven. But now he had something new on his mind, something horrible, yet something he deserved, which was that if Epp died, Klaus would be stuck arranging the funeral. When Epp's uncle Walter died two years ago, Epp had had to take care of the funeral, and he came to Klaus for help.

"You intend to embalm him?"

"You mean pickle the bugger?"

"Preserve him," said Klaus.

"What for?"

"Looks."

"I know what the old bastard looked like."

"I thought you were an orphan."

"He's not a real uncle, he's a sorta uncle."

"A friend."

That didn't seem to be the right word either. "A big brother. You know that organization, Big Brothers. He used to come around."

"And he named you executor of his estate."

"What?"

"So what are you going to do?"

"Jesus, Klaus, you tell me."

Klaus got out the Yellow Pages and the next day they were in Green Grove Funeral Home sitting on a French Provincial couch sipping tea from bone china as translucent as skin. The undertaker was a young Chinese guy named Andrew Song, who had a complexion as perfect as a white plastic bag. He gave Epp a brochure titled "Helpful Information About Funerals." A silhouette on the cover showed a man seated on a garden bench in deep reflection upon the eternal. Epp took it like the last card in a losing hand. He placed it alongside a pamphlet on grieving, a step-by-step cost breakdown, and a booklet titled "Your Funeral and You." He looked around the room. Dried flowers stood in vases, the wallpaper was a shade of green intended to soothe, and there were chairs and tables.

"Could almost live here," said Epp.

"I do."

In the silence that lay like dropped pants Klaus and Epp studied Mr. Song with new regard.

Epp said, "Here?"

"Upstairs." Andrew Song had clearly dealt with this before and took them both on with a frank gaze. He had the eyes of a man with access to back rooms, and as for his eyebrows they were nearly nonexistent, which lent him the eerie appearance of an alien. "Can you tell me something about the deceased? That might help you decide on the style of service."

Epp shoved the fan of literature forward as if laying down his cards. "He was a asshole."

Mr. Song maintained his unrippled gaze. "Was he a Christian?"

Epp nodded deeply. "Last I knew he went to church, yeah."

"And he expressed no preferences concerning final arrangements?"

Klaus watched Epp work over the question. "He didn't talk about death?"

"Always, just not his."

Mr. Song cleared hs throat. "Essentially, your options are cremation or burial."

"Which is cheapest?"

"Cremation."

"Okay." Epp sat back, hoping it was over.

"But you'll still have to select a casket."

The casket display room resembled a ghoulish boarding house. The caskets were arranged like open beds atop tube metal stands with silk and satin pillows propped and waiting. The carpet had a moist and rotting richness. Klaus tried not to breathe too deeply. Epp, on the other hand, whistled in admiration and went right up to a casket of lacquered and inlaid oak and placed his palm on it.

"How much does one of these babies go for?"

"That one is eight thousand dollars."

Epp's hand leapt as if scorched.

"That's our Canadian Confederation Casket. Twelve woods and veneers representing the provinces and territories, including oak, birch, maple, cedar, fir, pine, and dogwood. Solid brass fittings, shirred satin interior, jumbo cushion, spring mattress, tuck and groove walls and ceiling." Mr. Song folded back the pleated fringe exposing a rubber gasket along the upper and lower edges. "This is Durotec. It comes with a seventy-five-year guarantee to seal out all moisture and particles." He reached under the pillow and held up a gold key on a chain and inserted it into a lock at the casket's foot. "The key provides peace of mind against disturbance."

Epp's eyes widened like a boy hearing a tale. "You mean like grave robbers?"

Andrew Song let that pass. He observed Epp from the austere remoteness of professional decorum. "All our cemeteries have twenty-four-hour security."

"Eight grand and you just burn the bugger." Epp

looked to Klaus, inviting him to share the mystery of it all. Then he wandered deeper into the room gazing at the open caskets. "How about that one?"

Mr. Song became faintly impatient, like a waiter who'd pegged them for lousy tippers. "Eighteen gauge lead-coated steel. Twelve thousand dollars."

They looked at the coved and gleaming lid of polished metal as if admiring the hood of a vintage car.

"Perhaps over here." He led them to a stack of cloth-covered caskets in the far corner. The one on the bottom was plain particle board. "One hundred and ninety-five dollars. Your basic burning box."

"I coulda knocked that together in an hour. Hey Klaus, you got those sheets of plywood. We could make one." Epp turned. "We'll bring our own."

Mr. Song's manner remained as smooth and cool as that steel-coated casket. "I'm afraid not."

Epp argued, but Mr. Song stood firm on this point of company policy. Then his beeper went off and he excused himself.

"Just pay with the money you inherit," said Klaus.

"He was in debt."

"How the hell did you get roped into this?"

"I told you. He gave me a place to stay when I left the orphanage. Got me my first job. I owe him."

When Andrew Song returned, he relented a little, "You are perfectly free to provide your own urn."

Nonetheless, he directed them toward glass display shelves.

Epp put his fists in his back pockets and scanned the selection of jars and vases. There were even sets of small matching urns for families wishing to share out the ashes. Epp gestured with his chin. "How about that one?" Mr. Song lifted a jug of dark marble and offered it. Epp's eyebrows jumped at its weight. "Feels like a goddamn bowling ball. How much?"

Mr. Song consulted the card. "Fourteen."

"Bucks?"

"Hundred."

Epp blew out his cheeks and studied the urn with new respect. "How about that bugger?" He indicated a plain brown cylinder with a screw top.

"Plastic. Ten dollars."

Even with a ten dollar plastic urn and a particle board burning box, the funeral came to eight hundred and forty dollars. Klaus went along the day Walter was cremated. On the way home, the urn containing the ashes sat on the backseat of Epp's '74 Duster.

"Looks kind've sad back there," said Epp.

"Bring him up here."

But Epp didn't. Instead, he started talking about Walter. "Open season on Chinks'n Hindus. That's what he used to say when he went to the rifle range. Open season on Chinks'n Hindus."

Klaus had watched Epp. "A liberal, was he."

"Naw, always voted Social Credit. What he really liked doin' is shootin' airplanes. He had the schedule, see. These big bloody jets coming in like goddamn battleships. He'd drive along the freeway right underneath them and take pot shots. He could do that 'cause he had a convertible. Every Saturday at noon when the Hong Kong flight was coming in."

"Did he ever get caught?"

"Had a silencer. Used to take me with him and I'd hold the steerin' wheel.

"Get out of here."

"I'm tellin' you."

"How old were you?"

"Ten."

Klaus had looked out the side window at the black and barren trees of February and thought of burnt bones. "This Walter sounds like he was dangerous."

"Naw. Silencer cuts the punch way down."

"So you know about guns, do you?"

Epp drove on not wanting to talk about it. It was the only time Klaus ever knew Epp to be enigmatic. "I told you, I was ten."

§

As Wong led his own funeral procession back to the

office, Hunt paused by Klaus and raised his camera.

"You mind?"

"You a cop?"

Hunt liked that. "Head office."

"Well, I do mind."

Hunt lowered the camera. His grin faltered only for a second before climbing back into place. "Okay, buddy."

Mutton appeared at Klaus's side. "How 'bout takin' my picture?"

Hunt studied Mutton as if looking through the bars of a cage. "Sure."

Mutton struck a beauty queen pose and batted his lashless eyes.

Thinking of the boys Back East, Hunt snapped the shot, and headed for the office.

Klaus set another pan on the tractor tread that led to the oven, and said to Mutton, "What do you think?"

"Kinda cute in a nasty fashion."

"I mean Epp."

"He's a runt. Runt's are hard as roaches." In his time at sea, Mutton had seen many of Epp's type on ship, all of them unkillable. He recalled Isaac Fly, a Trinidadian of black, white, and Chinese background. Fly was so bowlegged the sailors maintained that a blind man could've pissed between his knees. Despite his skills at soccer and ping pong, Fly, like Epp, was accident prone. He'd lost half an ear when a sheet metal heat duct dropped from the galley wall in heavy seas south of Cape Town. He regularly smashed his thumb chipping rust. He fell overboard one night in the Red Sea and spent eleven hours with the garbage sharks. In Rio, a whore stabbed him in the right buttock with a fork, and he'd caught cholera in Bombay. Fly's luck ran out in San Francisco when he got run over by a streetcar.

"Maybe Epp's luck's run out."

"Not when he could jump off your roof like that."

Klaus managed a laugh. Epp liked jumping off things. When Klaus and Darlene bought the house across from Fraserview Cemetery, Epp insisted on jumping out of their living room window as a sort of housewarming ritual. After he did the window, he said he'd jump off their roof, but it would cost fifty bucks. Klaus offered twenty. Everyone at the bakery signed Epp's cast.

Klaus tried feeling encouraged. "You really put the boots to Keegan last night."

"Place can close tomorrow for all I care. I'll be on the beach in Cuba sipping Penis Coladas." Then Mutton's tone took on a feigned innocence. "How's yer darlin' Darlene?"

Klaus shrugged. "Fine." He didn't mention that today was their twentieth wedding anniversary.

"Saw her, when was it . . . last weekend. Saturday. Saturday night."

"She shops Saturday night after work."

"Does, does she?"

"Yeah."

"Was with a woman."

The belt shunted the pans forward and Klaus continued loading, each inflated dough lying delicate as an infant in its pan. "Sylvia."

Again Mutton nodded. "Sylvia. Is that right."

"Yup."

"Good mates are they?"

Klaus shrugged. "Women."

"Just wonderin'."

"Uh huh."

"It bein' Salome's, an' all." Mutton's tone was breezy and offhand.

"Salome's."

Mutton suddenly discovered the clock. "Shite, look-it that. Me coffee break."

Klaus watched Mutton beeline for the coffee room. Salome's was a gay bar. Darlene had met Sylvia about a year ago. Sylvia had come into Western Drugs where Darlene cashiered and, so Darlene described it, traded some banter over brand names—Kotex, Tampax, Javex, Windex, Gortex, Brand X—and they ended up going for a coffee. Sylvia was a few years older, divorced, had short hair and was as solid as a stack of bricks. Klaus had met her only once, just after moving down into the basement. He came home from The Blue Boy one Saturday night and there she was by the furnace gunning his weedwacker.

"Klaus, this is Sylvia, is it okay if she borrows—"

Klaus had grabbed it. "You're not supposed to use it inside. It's gas. There's exhaust. It's like running a car indoors. Carbon monoxide. Ever heard of it?" Klaus threw open the basement door. "And you're smoking a cigarette. Great."

"I'd worry more about the fumes coming off your breath," said Sylvia. "You're the fire hazard."

Ever since then Klaus feared Sylvia. And he knew what she was thinking: that he was keeping Darlene down. Sylvia knew he was sleeping on an army cot in the basement. Klaus could just hear Sylvia's second-rate psychologizing. *He's hiding because he can't face you. He can't even face himself. That's why he's a drunk. He'd rather wither up and die. And he's going to take you down too. Leave him.*

Would she? It had to be on Darlene's mind. Why stay? After all, Darlene had a job, and their daughter Odette was seventeen and on her own. Why stick around with a drunk who lived in the basement?

Loading the oven, Klaus wondered how much time he had before she left. One month? Six? A year? Or maybe, in her heart, she'd already left.

§

When Keegan and the cops left, Hunt invited Wong up to Wong's own office. Wong climbed the steps as if climbing to the gallows. They took seats on opposite sides of Wong's desk. Only now did Wong notice the three long claw marks down Hunt's cheek. The camera still hung from his neck. Inside it were multiple shots of the toppled forklift, the barricade of trays Epp had hidden behind, and Wong himself.

Hunt tried not to smile. "Wongo."

Wong envisioned Hunt in the Toronto boardroom delivering his report on the conditions in the Vancouver plant, which the senior managers would pass on to the lions in New York. "What's going to happen?"

Hunt blew air. "You tell me." Again Hunt tried not to smile. "You got a man overboard, cops all over, a shit-load of bad PR, and one pissed off union."

Wong clenched his jaw so tight his molars hurt.

Hunt checked his watch. "I'm flying down to Seattle this afternoon."

Wong didn't need to ask why.

"This is all good news to them. More work, more jobs."

Wong was about to lean his head in his hands, but stopped himself. He refused to collapse in front of anyone, especially Hunt. Then Wong noticed those scars on Hunt's face again. "What happened to your face?"

Hunt smiled. "Sushila loves sex."

CHAPTER SIX

A Blonde Wife

SINGH FINALLY ESCAPED THE BAKERY just in time for the Friday afternoon traffic. Yet while the other commuters suffered, caged and cursing in their dirt-glazed cars, he drove with the indifference of the defeated, slouched in his bucket seat, hands draped over the bottom of the steering wheel, thinking of his younger brother Bulgit, who'd just sent a letter from Chandigarh where he was discovering his roots. Singh remembered Chandigarh as a vast construction site of sand and cement and dust. To him, India was bearded men, and mountainous auntijis soft as feather-filled cushions. Singh arrived in Vancouver at the age of five. Bulgit was born three months later, and put great emphasis in having been conceived in India. Conception was the vital point, delivery only a technicality. And though his mother, who'd endured a thirty-hour delivery, didn't quite agree, she never said much because Bulgit was not a listener. A snapshot had accompanied the letter: Bulgit in beard and turban, kara on his wrist and kirpan in his sash. Bulgit had been called Bill in school, just as Singh, whose name was Patwant, was Pat. But in university, Bill became Bulgit again, and began spending time in the gurdwara. Pat laughed at him almost as hard as he laughed at the New Age whiteys who wore turbans. When Bulgit announced his trip to India, Pat told him be sure to have a drink with their uncle Dhalip.

"Every afternoon he'd grease his arm in ghee, lift the cow's tail, and shove his hand inside and come out with a bottle of Scotch. It was like a magic trick."

Bulgit gave him the hard eye. "You think that's funny, don't you."

"The cow seemed to like it."

"You're lucky you're my brother."

"I say a prayer of thanks every day."

"To who? You're a Godless atheist."

"I'm a pantheist. God's in everything."

"The only God you worship is the TV."

"Oh, Baba Looie, forgive me."

"That's all it comes down to isn't it, watching white trash slap hockey pucks and punch each other's teeth in."

"Listen to the knife-packing pacifist on his soap box."

"You know the really sad thing?"

"I can't wait to hear."

"An honours degree in political science and you waste your time in that factory full of monkeys. Five years of university and you work graveyard counting loaves of bread. What the fuck happened to you?"

Singh recalled the tears of anger in his brother's eyes. He also knew it was theatre, sincere theatre, but theatre nonetheless. He'd seen Bulgit in action all through childhood. Bulgit had one speed and one direction, fast forward. He was a "cause man." And the women fought over him. That briefly motivated Singh to talk the talk as well, but they saw through him. Pat would rather talk goalkeeping than Khalistan. And as for this battle about chairs in the temple, Pat Singh found it embarrassing. Whenever it was in the paper or on the box, he groaned.

At work it was worse, because he had to put up with remarks by guys like Stahl. Singh knew Stahl had wanted the supervisor position. He even saw his gripe. Stahl had put in his time and he knew every step of the process from scaling to mixing to wrapping to shipping. Stahl was the most qualified man on the shop floor, which was why they kept him there as production foreman. There was only one thing Stahl didn't know, which was that you should never get good at something you didn't want to do, because the powers that be will make you do it. Stahl, in his bitterness at Singh, was guaranteed to make some comment whenever Indo-Canadians were in the news. When an Indian newspaper editor got gunned down, Stahl said good. When the police closed the Ross Street gurdwara, he said good. When Sikh conservatives and moderates fought, he laughed at the ragheads and said ship 'em back where they came from. Bulgit would have punched Stahl out; Pat pretended not to hear.

To Pat Singh, Vancouver was a city of teams. There was the Chinese team, the German team, the Italian team, the Sikh team, the Muslim team, the Hindu team. Lately there were Iranian, Latino, and Somali teams, too. And they were all in competition.

Almost home, he swung the Volvo into Canton Crescent—the blacktop as perfect as paint, the lawns like carpets—and then into the gleaming driveway and right on up into the garage. He hit CLOSE on the automatic door control. Nothing. He pressed it again. The scroll door stayed open. He felt frustration trying to flare through his fatigue. Fuck it. He got out.

He lived in Richmond, the fancy name for Lulu Island, a swampy delta formed by the North and South arms of the Fraser River. Richmond had become Vancouver's new Chinatown. Enter Aberdeen Mall and you entered Hong Kong. The preferred theory went that the Chinese liked Richmond because it contained the word "rich." The Knight Street Bridge spanned the North Arm of the Fraser connecting Richmond to Vancouver. It was the butt of a joke: What's the longest bridge in the world? The Knight Street Bridge—it goes from Vancouver to Hong Kong.

Singh stood by the Volvo's back bumper where some wag had written WIPE MY REAR END in the mill dust on the trunk. He reached to pull the garage door shut, but it stayed stuck. He stepped up onto the bumper, got the handle with both hands, then gave it all his weight. It broke and rattled down on top of him. He lay on his back with the door across his stomach. It didn't hurt. The flimsy aluminum door was as light as an aluminum pie plate, more alarm system than barricade—one touch and it boomed like theatre thunder. So he simply lay where he was, the lower half of his body inside the garage and his torso outside. He noted how chilly the cement was under his butt and yet how pleasantly warm the sun-heated tar of the new driveway was under his back. He watched clumps of cloud sail up from the southwest and gather against the mountains on the North Shore. Yes, it really did rain less in Richmond. Pouring in town and dry here. Five miles made all the difference. Singh closed his eyes and felt the blood slowly flowing toward his head due to the driveway's incline. Maybe he should

start doing yoga like Bulgit, who stood on his head twice
a day. When Pat had reminded him yoga was a Hindu
and not a Sikh practise, Bulgit said no, it was an Indian
practise, and that was exactly the sectarian thinking that
caused all the problems.

"You okay?"

Singh twisted and saw Benny Chow at the end of
the driveway, walking his three prize-winning siamese
cats. "In the pink."

"Wha'?"

Singh said, "In, the, pink." He interlaced his fingers
behind his head for a pillow and got comfortable. "How
are Win, Place, and Show?"

Chow looked at his cats. "Win got diarrhoea."

Blood filling his head, Singh tried remembering the
last time he'd got drunk or had a toke. He hadn't
smoked a joint since the last time he saw B.B. King, and
he'd missed the last two concerts. That meant nearly
three years. Singh had seen B.B. King eleven times, the
first time in 1981 at U.B.C., on a double bill with Jerry
Lee Lewis. *"Wine, wine, wine. Pass that bottle to me."* Now
Singh tried remembering where his harmonica was. The
front door opened and he heard a scream. His reaction
was to toss a jaunty wave to show he was fine. His
mother stood with her hands over her mouth while his
wife rushed down the steps and helped him sit up.

"They've grown."

"Who?"

Singh pointed to the row of 18-inch junipers that Ute had planted beneath the front window last week. "Your hedge."

His mother stood over him cracking her knuckles, a habit that made Singh grit his teeth.

"Ma. Stop it."

§

Singh's mother Kamala coached Ute through the preparation of a bowel-burning biryani that evening. Seven months pregnant, Ute was the same shape as her mother-in-law. Ute also wore the same baggy pants and long shirt, plus the bangles and anklets. The only difference was Ute's blonde hair. Ute was from Munich. She'd converted to Sikhism against Pat's wishes, and against his wishes they'd had a traditional marriage. Singh lived in secret fear that she'd even take on his mother's accent.

After supper, Ute said they were going to the gurdwara. Ute was now a devout Sikh. She even took the name Kaur, as all Sikh women do, meaning princess.

Singh took the sports page to the couch. "Have fun."

The two women glared accusingly in their overcoats. It had clouded over and begun to rain.

133

"You look like a couple of buffalos."

Ute gave him the finger, using her belly as a screen from her mother-in-law who'd be appalled. Singh's mother began cracking her knuckles.

"Ma. You'll have fingers like lobster claws."

"It's nerves," said Ute, implying that if Singh came to the gurdwara his mother wouldn't be so anxious and would therefore stop cracking her knuckles. His mother had moved in when his father died.

When they were gone, Singh went to bed. He hadn't mentioned Epp or Keegan or the fact that he'd probably take the rap if Epp drowned. He just let them think he'd done six hours overtime. It gave him a grim and masochistic satisfaction keeping it to himself. What else was he good for? He bore the burdens. And if they threw him to the jackals now he'd live on in their guilt-riddled memories, a martyr immortalized by a generous life insurance policy. The goalkeeper, that's what he was, the goalkeeper, the one who made all the saves, the one it all came down to, the one everyone relied upon. His dream had been to be the first Sikh goalie in the NHL.

Singh and Ute had been married two years. Her first boyfriend, in Munich, had been a Tamil refugee. Since then there'd been Cambodians, Algerians, Turks, and a Bush Negro from Surinam. Singh met her through Bulgit. Bulgit didn't want her; he wanted an Indian wife, so Singh got Ute on the rebound. His parents were relieved and disappointed. Ute was three years older than Bulgit and that would have been unnatural. Pat, on the other hand, was the oldest, so should marry first. True, she was white, but at least she was German, a good white, not a crazed Slav or irrational Irishman. Pat was short and jowly and dour, and had never done well with women. Marriage made him more confident. He could now sit with the uncles and cousins and enjoy the status of lying between the legs of a blonde woman, the fantasy of every male, black, brown, white or yellow, no matter what malarkey they made up. He'd satisfied all the basic requirements and more: good job, blonde wife, big house, baby on the way. Now the rellies could busy themselves stabbing him in the back for other things, the fact that he wasn't devout. And when Ute gave birth to a girl—as the ultrasound showed she would—there would be the usual false sympathy.

Sometimes he understood Dhalip hiding that bottle up the cow's ass. Yes, wait'll little bro' got a snootful of Mother India. The letters so far though were disappointingly cheerful. The little prick was having a good time. Pat, too, once wanted to "go back." Every Indian knew what it meant. And a few had done it. The old mostly. Singh felt sorry for them, especially when he saw them wandering the streets of Vancouver, or sitting on bus benches but not waiting for buses, and so piss-ing off the drivers who pulled in. He saw them sitting on gas station retaining walls watching the traffic as if they'd never seen cars before, as if Sikhs didn't dominate Delhi's taxi industry. He saw them bewildered in shopping malls. He saw them in the rain, wearing vegetable bags over their turbans. And he saw them stranded in the traffic islands of busy streets, unable to get all the way across, yet unable to get back, which nearly made him cry. Singh's own grandparents had both died within two years of arriving in Vancouver. He and his grandfather had had a game in which Pat swung from the old man's beard, the old man laughing and swaying his head side-to-side while little Patwant hung on, shrieking in delight.

Unable to sleep, Singh got up and wandered the house. Eighteen thousand dollars worth of as-yet-unpaid-for Kashmiri carpets alternated with blonde oak floors. There were hammered brass plates leaning on the mantel, embroidered cushions, Naga shawls, a brass and porcelain hookah with six silk-wrapped leads, and hallucinogenic portraits of blue-skinned saints. There was a three-by-four foot photo of the Golden Temple, the lake palace of Udaipur, the medieval vista of Varanasi at dawn showing the thousands bathing in the Holy Ganga. Pat had made one contribution—his three-legged pine sidetable from Grade Nine Woodwork—which kept finding its way out to the garage. If he took the fall for this Epp business everything would go. Singh, always inclined toward the negative, could already hear his mother shrieking and cracking her knuckles. And now this guy Hunt was around. Singh didn't like the way the guy smiled, one of those Upper Canada WASPS with chlorine-coloured eyes and scar tissue skin. He could sense it all stacking up against him. Who had the black mark? Him. All over his face. Except, of course, Singh was no darker than Wong or any Italian or Portuguese you could point to. And perfect timing: new house, no job. Yes, he'd provide the rellies fodder for years to come if Wong pinned this on him. Of course, they'd be outraged on his behalf, they'd cry racism, but secretly they'd be delighted. More fuel for the fire.

It was now nine P.M. Singh had gone right around the clock to what was, for him, morning. Wong knew how long Singh had been on shift, but had kept him there anyway. The Ayatollah Wong. Three years Singh had been on graveyard. Did he complain? He went to work when everyone else went to bed, and went to bed when they went to work. Maybe he should have given Epp the six A.M. moulder shift. Anyone could handle that. Twenty-two years and still dumping flour. Singh's back began to ache from falling off the Volvo's bumper. In the living room, Singh stood naked beneath the chandelier, raised his arms, and willed the thing to drop and kill him. Let them find him crushed by fake diamonds. He lowered his arms and looked down. That hard-on was back again.

CHAPTER SEVEN

City Nights

SINGH WOULD SWING. Stahl liked that. And he decided to help hang him. When Stahl's shift ended at two in the afternoon, he left the bakery and drove to Canadian Tire. He bought a combination lock, which he took care to scuff up by scraping against the sidewalk. Then he hit the liquor store on Main near the McDonald's. He bought a mickey of the cheapest rye he could find, Black Velvet, then crossed to McDonald's and used the can, took a long swig of the rye, then went and bought a plain burger and sat in a corner watching the girls. Chinese ones wobbling around on block-soled shoes, East Indian ones with big knockers and moustaches, pale white ones with red lips and insolent eyes.

By 3:05, McDonald's was claustrophobic with kids. They took seats nearby, eyeing Stahl as they did so, and, he was certain, discussing him. The girls leaned together to giggle and sneer in the new-found power of their sexuality. He bet it'd be different if he had blond hair. He bet if it was Bell, they'd be posing for him. He left. On his way out to his van, he discovered three guys huddled between it and the liquor store wall. Two whirled and walked away. The third moved more slowly. When Stahl reached the van door, the kid stood only a few yards off. He looked about eighteen, had a goatee, and wore a faded jean jacket felt-penned with crucifixes. His lingering like that made Stahl worry. Stahl gripped the bottle tighter, thinking he'd have to slug the kid with it, or Christ, who knew, maybe the kid was in a gang and had a gun. Stahl glanced around and saw he was trapped between the wall and his own van. The little bastards, they'd lured him in and now they had him. Despite his fear, part of him stayed calm, and he thought: Wasn't it always like that? Sudden? A car crash, a stroke, or they kick you to a pulp behind a liquor store?

"Up or down?"

"Huh?"

The kid watched Stahl. "Hash, pot, 'D.A.?"

"'D.A.?"

Reaching inside his jacket, the kid stepped closer

while Stahl stared at his haircut, one of those shaved-up-the-sides jobs with the top draped back like a slab of raw meat. The kid came out with a flap of tinfoil.

"Twenty-five."

Stahl glanced around, an idea forming. "Good?"

"Knock your head off."

Stahl had only a twenty and a ten.

The kid was brisk. He gave him the flap and five loonies. "Need a rig?"

Stahl had no idea what he was talking about. He heard his own voice say, "No."

"Okay. Have a good one."

"Yeah. Yeah, you too."

And just like that, Sourdough Stahl had made his first dope deal.

He parked two blocks from the bakery and carefully unfolded the tinfoil. The stuff looked like Dutch Cleanser. He sniffed at it. No smell. He wet the tip of his baby finger and dabbed up a few grains and tasted it. Bitter. He felt oddly unimpressed. He folded it up and put it in his pocket. It was raining now, but the clouds were broken, their cracks revealing a marbling of blue. Spring rain, spiced with the acrid scent of weeds sprouting from the seams in the sidewalk. Carrying his gym bag, he walked quickly but casually, and even began whistling as he turned the corner coming into full view of the lot in case someone spotted him. No one did.

There was Epp's Duster. There was Wong's Jaguar. He went up the same steps Epp had dashed down that morning, in through the door, and straight on between the high walls of cardboard boxes containing bread bags, and, pausing to listen for voices in the coffee room, turned right then left and pushed open the change room door and stopped. The lockers ran along both walls. There was Bell's, there was Klaus's. Few guys actually bothered locking their lockers. Mutton didn't. Stahl, however, did. And so did Singh. Stahl listened again. Nothing. He went to Singh's locker, opened the gym bag and took out a set of bolt cutters. He squatted and clamped his knees around the arms of the cutters for extra leverage and snipped the lock. He opened the door, wincing at the stink of Singh's sweat-rotted boots, and placed the mickey inside. As he was about to add the flap of dope, the change room door swung open. Keegan.

"Where's Wong?"

Stahl stammered.

Keegan looked past him. "Wong . . . Wong!"

"In his office," said Stahl.

"Just looked."

Keegan had Lou Camponi, the union lawyer with him.

"Out back then."

"Back?"

"Yeah."

Keegan was about to turn and go when he frowned at Stahl. "You been off two hours. What're you doin'?"

Stahl stayed where he was, crouched before the locker, the bolt cutters hidden behind him on the floor. He lifted Singh's boots. "Forgot my boots."

But Keegan had already lost interest and was herding Camponi out. The door shut and Stahl was alone again. But his hands shook so badly now he couldn't find the new lock stashed in his gym bag. He watched his hands plunge about like panicked rats. Stahl finally got hold of the new lock, but before using it hesitated, glanced around, gobbed a big one into one of Singh's boots, then shut the door. A minute later he was outside walking away.

§

Keegan and Camponi found Wong on the loading dock, where he'd just finished supervising the salvage of the forklift. Four of the afternoon crew had tipped it upright, then driven it around to the ramp. It looked no worse for wear than any other forklift driven by hungover men on nightshift.

Seeing Keegan and Camponi, Wong said, "What the hell's this?"

"I'd call it a lawsuit," said Camponi.

Wong felt volts jolt his heart. Lawsuit. At this rate, Wong realized he could consider himself lucky if they sent him to Seattle. His life with Bestbuy was over. "You're on company property."

"Noncooperation," said Camponi, as if citing the first in a long list of charges. Camponi had only an inch of forehead between his hairline and eyebrows. He wore a red turtleneck sweater because red looked good with his black hair and olive skin. The sweater also hid his his paunch.

"Fine. We'll put that opposite the assault charge I'm bringing against the union." Wong saw Camponi's surprise. "Keegan didn't tell you about that little stunt last night, did he."

Keegan shouted, "I had nothing to do with those dough balls. It was a maverick act of violence, just like—" He was about to add it was just like Jimmy busting that cop's jaw. "There'll be an apology."

"An apology." Wong snorted. "It'll take a little more than that, Hank. I was attacked." In a moment of inspiration, he considered claiming that he'd been having headaches, but realized Keegan had seen him taking codeines, and that a lawyer would go to town on the fact that Wong's migraines preceded the assault. Still, he had one piece of evidence. He removed his glasses and showed Keegan the gouge in the lens. "Six hundred dollars, my friend. And a dozen witnesses."

"The union'll pay."

"You're damned right it will. Now get out."

§

Stahl didn't slow down until he was back in his van and the Friday afternoon traffic had absorbed him. He took his cell from the glove box, then put it back. No. A booth. He'd use a booth. He pulled over and called the police, eyeing the cars crawling past for anyone who might be taking too much notice of him. Yet the booth was too blurred with rain for him to be identified. He left his message, hung up, then rejoined the traffic, his wipers dropping side to side and his message repeating in his mind. Wait'll the cops check that out, he thought. Then he wondered when they'd get on it. Tonight? Monday? Probably Monday. Stahl pictured the cops trooping in Monday morning and demanding to see Singh's locker. Would they cuff him when they found the stuff? And once again, he remembered the cops arriving at the bakery and arresting him for assault. Graves had never said anything about that, but Stahl knew it was a mark against him, that that was another reason he'd been passed over for the supervisor position. Fine, thought Stahl. Let's see what a little visit from the cops does for Singh's future.

Stahl spent the next two hours visiting camera

shops. He wanted a telephoto lens, high powered, like spies used. Yet the prices: fifteen bills for the lens alone. And those lying bastard salesmen talking Built-in Speedlight, 3D Matrix Metering with D-type AF Nikkor . . . . He decided he'd wait until tomorrow morning. He was too anxious to buy now, so he continued driving around, the rain easing and the darkness deepening. Stahl often ran through two entire tanks of gas on his aimless evening drives. To Stahl, Vancouver was both familiar and foreign. It was a locked door. He'd studied it all his life, but still didn't know how to open it.

He stopped at Canadian Tire and bought flashlight batteries and a crowbar. The one innocent act of pleasure in Stahl's life was wandering the aisles of the various Canadian Tire stores. Car parts, hardware, cleaning products, lawn furniture, these things put him at ease. Browsing fuel filters and floormats and car wax, was the one pastime blessedly free of sexual connotations, the one place he could be on an afternoon or evening and it was okay. He knew all twenty-two locations. And by staggering his visits, he never became known as some loser who hung out in Canadian Tire.

Drugstores, on the other hand, were a problem. How could he approach some eighteen-year-old girl at the cash register with a pack of ribbed condoms? Or with Preparation H? Or, more to the point, with blond hair dye? Still, he spent as much time in drugstores as in

146

Canadian Tires. He lingered in front of the garbage bags, the razor blades, the magazines. Then he moved on to the shampoo, where he was within striking distance of the hair dye. He'd wait until the aisle was empty, then, a starved man staring in the window of a meat shop, he'd touch the tubes and sprays and bottles that could change his hair from mole-brown to blond, that could change his life from shit to sunshine. It was during one such session that a biker with black-rooted blond hair reached past him, grabbed a tube of Clairol, and said to Stahl, "Good shit, man." Chains swinging from his belt, he bowled on down the aisle to the cash register. Stahl had stared. Then, goddammit, he did the same. He even went to the same cashier, and, defiant, threw down a twenty and waited for his change. When he got home he bolted the door then went into the bathroom. At last. Yet he still faced the other problem: the guys at work. Show up blond they'd laugh at him. They'd peck him to death like a tainted bird. But he had to try the stuff out. He had to. So he dyed his pubic hair, and for the next six months John Stahl walked differently.

§

As he drove, Stahl wondered what had become of Donnelly. Stahl had heard he needed an operation, a couple of operations. He considered dropping into the hospital and seeing him, but Donnelly was another one who treated him like he had some kind of smell. Fucking Klaus. Stahl knew where Klaus lived, but that'd be too obvious. He drove on by Fraserview Cemetery and swung slowly past Epp's place. He wanted to stand in the room of a dead man.

The house was a 1950s box with stucco walls. Stahl parked at the end of the street and walked back up the sidewalk, flashlight in his pocket and iron crowbar cold under his coat. He cut in alongside the overgrown laurel. Stahl was as lean as a ladder, but still had to turn sideways to fit between the hedge and the wall. He stood beneath the back porch. The rain had stopped, but dripped from the eaves. He could see the lights of downtown reflected off the clouds like fire flickering on the ceiling of a cave. He heard a siren, the Fraser bus whining its way up the hill, and beyond it all the machine-roar of the city. Across the alley, kitchen lights glowed. People were at home having supper, playing cards, watching *Entertainment Tonight*. Under the porch, the world was wet wood, wet cement, wet garbage. Stahl felt forlorn. His leanness made him embarrassingly susceptible to chills. He shivered and hugged himself.

Then he tried the basement door. Locked.

He went around to the far side of the house, crouched at the ground-level bedroom window, and discovered it had bars. He also discovered he had to pee.

Hidden there between the wall and the fence, Stahl undid his pants. He was mid-whiz when the bedroom light snapped on. He staggered, spattering his leg and fighting with his zipper. Pressed flat to the wall, he waited, the stucco's grit biting his back, then he ducked and peeked in the corner of the window. It was curtained with a Canadian flag that didn't fall flush to the frame, so he could see a piece of Epp's bed, and on the wall a section of that weird picture of dogs dressed as English gentlemen at the dinner table. And there, in the outlet near the floor, Stahl recognized one of those timers that automatically switch on your lights. He had one himself. Did he dare break the window and pry out the bars? It wouldn't have been his first B&E, and not the first window he'd peeked into. The Urge had taken hold in his late teens. The erratic shifts at the bakery had been conducive. He'd get off work at midnight or two A.M. and then wander the streets. He'd peek into four, five, six windows a night until he found what he wanted. Not sex, no. Limbs locked and writhing made him think of snakes. What he liked was to watch people sleep, watch them breathe and turn and twitch, watch them helpless.

Epp had been helpless in the river.

Stahl hoped Epp was dead. Not just because Epp was the one who'd first called him Sourdough, but because it would be exciting, and because it wasn't Stahl's fault. Innocence: it was a rare and beautiful state, like being blond, like being an angel. Looking in Epp's window, Stahl remembered Epp's lizard. Epp had brought it to work to show everyone and it got loose. A few mornings later, Stahl spotted it behind the mixer and whacked it with a meal scoop. When he picked it up he discovered the lizard had a satisfying weight. Its body was dry and soft, its scaled hide as beautiful as a beaded purse. His mother had owned a beaded purse. He'd raised the reptile to his face and put his cheek to it. Then he hid it in the rag barrel, and all through his shift kept returning to look at it. He considered taking it to a taxidermist. Instead, he wrapped it in a dough and sent it through the oven.

Now Stahl studied Epp's bed, a four-poster, a bed for two, a bed for sex. Epp, the little bastard, had high hopes. Stahl had a single. He remembered that Lee broad Epp had lived with. He'd seen them at the flea market with all that leather underwear. She looked like she had Indian in her. When he heard she dumped Epp, Stahl was glad. He didn't like the idea of people having sex while he had to jerk off. When he masturbated he put the TV on loud in case the neighbours overheard. He suspected they talked about him. He nearly went mad when a young couple moved in next door. They did it every night. They did it in the mornings, in the afternoons, and once he walked in on them while they were doing it in the laundry room.

Other than the bed and the picture, Epp's bedroom was bare. Stahl stepped to the corner intending to have a go at prying open the basement door with the crowbar, but halted when he saw Klaus coming across the lawn from the alley. Gripping the crowbar like an axe, Stahl stepped back and watched Klaus.

CHAPTER EIGHT

A Walk Across the Cemetery

A N HOUR EARLIER THAT EVENING, the same cops who interviewed Klaus in the bakery showed up at his place. Darlene called him up from the basement and they sat in the kitchen, the first time in five days Darlene and Klaus had been in the same room. The sight of a Black Forest cake on the counter deepened Klaus's guilt over missing their anniversary. He used to make a Black Forest cake himself for the occasion.

Everyone looked exhausted, the cops at the end of a long shift, Darlene from a fight with their daughter Odette, and Klaus after the longest day of his life. The older cop, McNeil, breathed loudly through his moist red moustache.

153

"How long did you know Mr. Epp?"

"Twenty-five years."

"Did?"

They looked at Darlene. She had her arms crossed tightly across her buttoned-up cardigan.

"You said, 'Did.'"

"We found a body."

A door slammed in Klaus's mind.

"We haven't been able to locate any relatives. We need someone to make an identification."

Klaus nodded.

"So you don't know for sure that it's him," said Darlene. She crossed her arms tighter and held the collar of her cardigan closed.

McNeil consulted his paperwork. "You say he was approximately 5'3" and forty years old?"

"Yeah."

McNeil's eyebrows rose apologetically as he read the bad news in his notepad. "That fits." Then he looked to Klaus. "Monday at ten? City Coroner?"

Klaus may as well have been pronounced dead himself. The morgue? Monday?

They watched McNeil pack up his pad and pen, and then remember something. "Oh. Got this call an hour ago: 'If you want Epp, look in Singh's locker.' Singh. He's the night shift supervisor, is that correct?"

"Yeah."

"Did this Singh and Epp have any," McNeil hunted the right word, "conflicts?"

"Epp wanted off graveyard."

"And Singh had the authority to do that."

Klaus saw how this looked. "I guess."

Darlene and Klaus accompanied the cops to the door and watched them go out the metal gate between the cement lions. A cold breeze was cracking the clouds, revealing stars. When the cops were gone, Darlene and Klaus discovered themselves side by side.

Using Epp as an excuse to keep Klaus from withdrawing, Darlene asked, "What happened?"

Klaus stepped onto the porch and avoided her eyes. He explained everything, including the wage cut.

"Gee Klaus, thanks for telling me. When were you planning to let me in on that little detail? I mean, not that we have any special connection to each other or anything."

"I know what day it is."

Darlene said nothing, just hugged herself against the chill as Klaus stared at the cemetery across the street. Twenty years. Two decades. Odette had been by earlier and brought that cake. Klaus had heard them arguing.

"What were you two fighting about?"

"You want to know what we were fighting about? You. She blames me for you living in the basement. She blames me for you not coming up on our twentieth anniversary." Darlene spoke the last words through tears.

Klaus marvelled at the timing. The wage cut, the arson, Epp in the river, and their twentieth anniversary, all in twenty-four hours. He'd avoided and avoided and avoided until it all piled up. "It's not your fault."

"Is that supposed to make me feel better?"

"Well, it isn't."

"No?"

"No."

Darlene watched him. She knew she was beating a bruise but couldn't stop herself. "Then do something."

"On fifteen dollars an hour?" Klaus kept his eyes on the gravestones. After a silence, he said, "Mutton saw you and Sylvia. At Salome's."

Darlene waited one guilty second too long before responding. "We were having a drink, so what."

Klaus started walking.

"So what?"

Klaus kept going.

Darlene yelled, "Happy anniversary." Then she shut the door and leaned her forehead against it. She wished Sylvia was here.

Sylvia had dropped by that afternoon with two lattes. They sat at the kitchen table, Sylvia's dark blue power-suit adding to the imposing impression created by her fireplug figure and jowly face. She looked, Darlene thought, like Charles Laughton in drag. As for Darlene, she saw herself as Louise Lasser in *Mary Hartman, Mary Hartman*, thin and pale, sad and absurd, not sure how she'd reached the age of forty so soon.

"Fuck, I hate kids," said Sylvia.

"Noel?"

"Today he was skulking around the girls using a hand mirror to look up their skirts. Eleven and he needs a testosterone inhibitor." Sylvia hoisted herself onto one buttock, slipped a fart, sipped her latte, then shook her head. "They are interesting though, in a grotesque way. Like at recess. I'm looking out the classroom window, and there's Noel and his crew kicking Dylan—kicking him. Dylan is on the ground being kicked—and he's laughing. I mean I'm watching this, but before I can make a move Dylan is up and it's Brett's turn, and they're kicking him. And he's laughing!"

"And the girls?"

"Back-biting little sucks."

"But they don't kick each other."

Sylvia put on the voice of a prissy girl. "They'd get their red plastic shoes dirty." Swallowing a belch, Sylvia frowned. "Jesus. Those salami subs. So . . . " Sylvia's tone signalled a new topic. "What did you think?"

Darlene didn't need an explanation. "I don't know."

"You were having fun."

"I was drunk."

"Two martinis is not drunk."

"I hadn't eaten all day."

Sylvia didn't push. "Okay, you were drunk." On the wall beside them the Sunbeam Bread clock ticked loudly, the butter-blonde Sunbeam Bread Girl pictured behind the clock-hands smiling overtop of a slice of white bread that resembled a mattress. Klaus had got it for Odette. "There she is in all her milkmaid purity, the cheese-fed fraulein, virgin-icon of the masculine dream."

They gazed at the Sunbeam Bread Girl. Odette used to love that clock, but now hated it. The Sunbeam Bread Girl used to be her idol, her imaginary friend, the girl she wanted to be. Odette had begged Darlene to dye her hair blonde and do it up exactly like the Sunbeam Bread Girl's. Now Odette called her Heidi The Whole Milk Whore.

"Were you really drunk?"

"I don't know."

Sylvia checked the clock. "Well, I gotta head. So, tomorrow?"

"Sure."

"I've got some dynamite bud."

Now Darlene's smile was genuinely spontaneous. "I need it."

§

Darlene had been seeing a psychiatrist for the past year.

Sylvia came up occasionally, but mostly they talked about Klaus.

"Don't worry," said Doctor Yi. "Klaus'll go thirty more years as long as he sticks to beer. It's the hard stuff that kills them."

Was Yi suggesting Klaus might spend the next thirty years in the basement? Once, and only once, Darlene convinced Klaus to talk to Yi about the drinking and depression. Klaus hated the idea. But he knew he had to at least put on a show of making an effort or Darlene might leave him. So one afternoon after work, Klaus went to Yi's office. Klaus sat in a lavendar armchair and watched, from deep within the stockade of his skull, as Yi played Xs and Os on his blotter and asked questions.

"You must like Bestbuy."

"It's a good job."

Yi's brow contracted with concern, pretending to suddenly remember something. "I thought you wanted to open your own shop?"

"Nope."

Yi stroked a line through three Xs and waited, but Klaus didn't go on. So Yi regathered himself. Sitting back and looking at the poster of killer whales in Johnstone Strait as though for inspiration, Yi said, "Darlene was here last week."

"I know."

"She sat in that very chair and cried."

"Then she needs the Prozac, not me."

"But you're the one living in the basement."

"Have to live somewhere."

Yi exhaled loudly, making it clear Klaus was being both obstinate and immature. "You could be upstairs with your wife."

Five beers in him, Klaus merely studied his own fingers and wondered how Yi, who was thirty-five, expected Klaus to open up to, much less take advice from, a younger man. If Yi was as all-wise as he liked to think, he'd know that.

"Tell me about your father."

Klaus crossed his arms and looked at the ceiling. "Last time I saw him he was in a coffin."

"How did you feel?"

"Relieved."

"That his suffering was over."

"No, that he was dead." Klaus watched Yi make a note.

Klaus was twenty when his father's heart cramped up tight as a fist. He returned to Calgary to arrange the funeral and look at the old man one last time, to be able to watch him without fear, to satisfy a fascination and fix in his mind forever the image of what he did not want to become, the image of what he feared he might be. Klaus's mother had refused to come, so it was just Klaus and the coffin. He left his mother sitting in the living room with her tenth or twentieth cup of tea, and when he returned five days later with the ashes, she was in the same chesterfield chair gazing out the window. If she hadn't been wearing her other housecoat, Klaus would have thought she hadn't moved. Leaving the old man had done her in. She'd broken away for survival, then hadn't had anything left with which to live. It was the bomb shelter that finally drove her out.

"Hannah I do this for you and Klaus. What do you think it was that Bay of Pigs? I tell you it was a diversion. Those Russians they are stupid but not that stupid. They won't come from the south anyway. They'll come from the other end—Alaska. All the way down the coast. And you know where this World War III it will be fought? Figure it out. Vancouver. That's a deep-sea port. They want their U-boats there. But you think the Americans will let them? Like hell. The goddamn Americans want this war. It's their ticket to get B.C. So not on your life we are moving to the coast. Besides, I got customers who all these years they are loyal. And when people they are loyal to me I am loyal to them. Only thing that can reach us here is the fall-out. You know what is fall-out, Klaus?

"Kurt. Don't scare him like that."

"Klaus, tell me what is fall-out."

"Kurt!"

161

"Come on, Klaus. Fall-out. What is fall-out?"

"The bomb."

"Okay. Close enough. Now what do you do when the air raid siren it goes off?"

"Hide."

"Where?"

"Downstairs."

"See Hannah, I am learning him survival skills. That bakery someday it is his. A business, a future. That's a valuable thing. A business is like a tree, Hannah, you keep pulling it up and moving it around sooner or later it dies. Do you want to die, Hannah? I don't want to die. Do you want to die, Klaus?"

"Kurt!"

"Klaus, do you want to die?"

Klaus shook his head.

"Of course not. No one wants to die. That's why I make that bomb shelter downstairs. Four thousand sacks of sand. I use four thousand sacks of sand to reinforce those walls. There is food, water, blankets, even cards so we can play fish. Now let me tell you something about your father, Klaus. Let me tell you something. I would cut my legs off for you, cut them both off right here at the knees. See, right here, with a saw, a big saw. Do you know why?"

"Kurt, he's nine!"

"What does that mean he is nine? Nine, eight,

seven, six, five, you are never too young. I got only one rule and that is you are never too young. Now Klaus, what would I do for you? Tell me."

"Cut off your legs."

"Where? Draw a line."

"Kurt!"

Klaus drew an imaginary line across his father's knees.

"Good. That's good. I would cut off my legs because I love you. You hear, Klaus, I love you. Your father, he loves you."

Two weeks later Klaus and his mother were living in Vancouver. Klaus hated it. He missed his father. When he told his mother that she dropped a soup bowl on the floor. Klaus feared his father, but with him there was order to the world. In Vancouver life lost that order. And then there was the weather. They'd exchanged Calgary's dry blue skies for Vancouver's clay grey clouds. It was March. They went to look at the ocean, but all they saw was sewagey surf shoving kelp and foam onto the shore. The rain made Klaus's coat smell of damp dog fur, soaked his pants so they stuck to his knees, sopped his socks, and turned the world to mud.

Klaus joined the grade three class, where Miss Dell mispronounced his name: "This is Claws Mann." The class howled. When he corrected her, the class howled even louder. They barked: Raus! Raus! like Schultz on

Hogan's Heroes. After that he was known as Schultz, Santa Claus, and Klouse the Louse.

When Klaus finished the story, Yi said, "Good, good." Then he began another game of Xs and Os. "Did your father ever . . . touch you?"

Klaus sat forward and surveyed the blotter with his five-beer frown. "You can't be both Xs and Os. It's cheating."

"Did he?"

"No. Did your father touch you?"

"How much are you drinking a day?"

"Case, case and a half."

"That's a lot of beer."

"I make good money."

"And you like your job."

"Wouldn't do anything else."

"How's your sleep?"

Klaus hadn't slept a night through in a year. And when Yi inquired, casually, about his sex life, Klaus inquired, just as casually, about his.

This made Yi reconsider his blotter of Xs and Os as if saddened that he had to resort to his next remark. "Your wife puts kitty litter under your bed."

Klaus repeated the words to himself, drawing them out like a tape measure to read the meaning.

"You stink."

Klaus was amused. "Do I?"

"According to Darlene."

Klaus said, "Well, according to me, you're fat."

"I have a weight problem, yes," said Yi.

Klaus watched Yi's neck, which bloated doughishly over his white collar.

"But I'm on a diet and fitness program. What are you doing about your weight?"

"I'm big-boned."

"What are you, two-forty, two-fifty?"

Klaus looked off toward the poster of killer whales and tried appearing bored.

"Why don't you shower?"

"We don't have one."

"Bathe then."

"You know us *gwailos*. We have a tradition of stinking."

Yi liked that. He chuckled. He began a new game of Xs and Os.

When Klaus got home, Darlene asked how it went.

"Yi cheats at Xs and Os." Then Klaus went downstairs to his room and looked under his cot. Kitty litter. Two trays of it.

CHAPTER NINE

Collagen Injections

KLAUS SPENT HIS twentieth anniversary lying on his cot drinking cans of Becks that he slid, one-by-one, from the socks in his drawer. One can per sock. He bought socks by the ten-pack from Zellers. Grey work socks with cinnamon coloured stitching at the heel and toe. Every time he pulled a beer from a sock he saw that cinnamon stitching and thought of cinnamon buns.

Darlene loved Klaus's cinnamon buns. They caused delirium. They were a triumph. More than that, they were sexy. Klaus had seduced Darlene with his cinnamon buns one winter evening in 1974. They'd walked in the snow all afternoon, until Klaus asked if she was hungry.

She said yes, expecting to order out for pizza or Chinese. Instead, Klaus led her to his apartment and turned on the oven and started opening cupboards. Soon there was dough, then the smell of raisins and cinnamon and butter all baking together. He made Viennese coffee and they ate the cinnamon buns hot, unwinding them, inhaling the sweet scent and moaning at the glorious taste. Darlene ate three, then looked at her sticky fingers, at which point Klaus leaned across and licked them slowly, one by one.

She'd never known a man who baked. She liked the thickness of his wrists and the delicate certainty with which he shaped the dough. She liked the way the warm and rising dough resembled a naked body. The smell of yeast became sensual. Cinnamon buns became a form of foreplay. When Klaus baked his cinnamon buns, Darlene knew what was on his mind. She could judge Klaus's level of contentment by how often he baked. To wind down after a night shift, he'd bake before going to bed, where Darlene would be waiting for him.

But Klaus did nothing for their twentieth anniversary. Odette brought a Black Forest cake despite Darlene's wish to let the whole anniversary business pass. Ever since Odette moved out she'd been giving her mother woman-to-woman advice. Odette had shaved the left side of her head, dyed the rest of her hair blue and orange, pierced both eyebrows, tattooed her shoulder with buzzards on a branch, and, just to be aggravating, made a grand performance of smoking Turkish cigarettes and drinking blue martinis. Living on cigarettes and martinis had brought her weight down from one hundred and sixty pounds to one hundred and three. Odette's last visit, a week before, was typical: "Mother: you can't let your twentieth anniversary go by! Mother: he's turning into a troll down there! Mother: you need to get laid!"

"See that door? Talk to me like that you can use it."

Odette merely rolled her eyes as if there was no use even trying to talk. Then she'd added, in that smug singsong: "It's true, though."

"Two years ago you were still wearing bunny rabbit pyjamas! Now you're the Happy Hooker!"

Trimming her cigarette, Odette smiled. Then she strolled into the living room shaking her head at the decor. "Look at this. A blue landscape?" She stood before the painting above the blue floral couch. Years it had been there, but only now did she comment on it. "Blue trees, blue farmhouse, blue horse. Jesus Christ, it's almost as bad as that stupid Sunbeam Bread clock."

Darlene pointed out that the picture matched the curtains. "And don't swear."

Once again Odette made with that aggravating shake of the head.

Odette was into The Doors. She'd read everything there was on Jim Morrison. She studied his lyrics and fantasized over his face. When Darlene told her she'd seen The Doors here in Vancouver, back in '67, Odette's eyes went blank with boredom. She didn't want her mother anywhere near The Doors. Odette secretly bemoaned having been born a generation too late to see The Messiah in person. The sixties had been wasted on people like her parents.

"No one who'd ever really *listened* to The Doors could hang a $29 blue landscape on her wall."

That was last week.

This afternoon, she'd arrived with the Black Forest cake just minutes after Sylvia had left. Darlene hadn't mentioned to Sylvia that this was her and Klaus's anniversary. And so far she'd managed to keep Sylvia and Odette from meeting. Darlene knew Odette would size Sylvia up and come to all kinds of conclusions. Darlene hated Odette's conclusions. When Odette came in she sat down at the kitchen table with that manner of hers, that little smirk that Darlene recognized from when she was seventeen—the absolute conviction that she was the only mature person in the universe. Odette sat there as if fatigued by the enormous burden of such maturity, one eyebrow arched, following Darlene's movements with patient indulgence, for after all, her forty-year-old mother was in her dotage. Odette's elbow rested on the table and she held her cigarette in a hand cocked back behind her ear. It was five-thirty and Klaus, who finished his shift at two, wasn't home.

"Maybe he left you."

"He's at The Blue Boy."

"Is that hamburger?"

"Yes."

"I don't eat red meat."

"You smoke cigarettes."

"I don't inhale."

"You'll get lip cancer."

"Not if I wear lipstick."

"Then you'll get tongue cancer and have to learn sign language."

"Judy's getting collagen injections."

"Why?"

"Because her lips are too thin. She's got no lips. Like there's skin, then it just ends. Her sister's going into nursing, and she said like if you've had an accident and your lips get cut off, they can make a graft from your asshole because it's the same."

"Why do you talk like that?"

"It's science!"

Darlene recalled Odette barfing in Grade 9 biology when they had to dissect a cow's eye, but didn't bother reminding her.

"Why don't you get rid of this thing?"

Darlene looked over from the stove. "You idolized the Sunbeam Bread Girl."

"Mother. I was nine."

"Yes. You're so mature now."

Odette narrowed her eyes. "Judy's mother's on Prozac."

"With a kid like Judy I'm not surprised."

"I'm gonna tell her that."

"Good."

Odette dragged on her cigarette then glanced at her watch.

Darlene had noticed the new watch right away, but refused to say anything.

Odette made a show of adjusting it.

Darlene kept her eyes on the cutting board where she was chopping onions. Odette borrowed $200 last month and it wasn't supposed to go on a watch.

"Well. Whataya think?" Odette turned her wrist in the light. "Lenny gave it to me."

Darlene let a few strategic moments pass before asking, casually, "And who's Lenny?"

"Just this guy."

Odette, having finally snagged her mother's interest, ducked behind a vague comment. Darlene thought it was a stylish watch, not gaudy and cheap like all the amulets and rings and other sixties trash Odette wore. This Lenny must be older. If the guy was getting down to business that might be just what she needed. Darlene recalled how, when she met Klaus, she was all over the place. She'd had two abortions, was just back from Mexico, and had no idea what to do next. Klaus had seemed so sober and stable then.

The sound of the Rabbit pulling into the carport stopped all talk. Darlene and Odette looked at each other. Odette parted the blue plastic venetians and narrated her father's progress.

"He's crossing the yard . . ." She stood, straining to see straight down. "Now he's going downstairs . . . " She turned, mouth open, and listened. They both heard the basement door open then quietly shut.

Odette asked the big question: "So, like, is he gonna come up and eat with us?"

Darlene turned away and tested the tomato sauce. The tartness stung her tongue, so she added sugar. Darlene knew Odette talked about her. She probably said how her parents were all fucked up—in just those words, too: all fucked up. She might even be laughing as she said it, shaking her head in that way she had and vowing no way man, that'd never happen to her.

"Well?"

"Well what?"

"Is he gonna eat with us?"

"Go ask him."

"You ask him. He's your husband."

173

Darlene turned, spoon dripping sauce. "And he's your father!"

"So?"

"So the anniversary party was your idea."

"You mean he's not coming up for his own twentieth anniversary?"

"No." Darlene's tone made her sound as if she was defending Klaus's wisdom. Turning away she rapped the wooden spoon so sharply on the edge of the pan the spoon broke. She stared at the jagged point. Klaus's plodding Germanness had seemed as sure and solid as a slow-moving train when she'd met him. What she hadn't realized was that the train was heading into a tunnel.

§

After supper Odette asked, "You got any condoms?"

Darlene sat in front of the TV watching a dung beetle roll what looked like a wad of black hash up a sand dune in Namibia. That's what she needed, a toke. She began clicking through the stations. "What do you want to do, blow them up and decorate?" She passed that beetle again rolling that ball of hash, and thought of Nepalese temple balls, which brought back memories of Kathmandu, Pig Alley, Freak Street, the women with hands like bricklayers and teeth red from betel nut. Those months in Nepal had been the best of her life. Or so she liked to think, even though she'd nearly died there of diarrhea, and Klaus, homesick, had almost left her.

"I want to be prepared."

Watching the images pop past, Darlene muttered, "Why would I have a condom?" She'd bought a sari in Nepal. When she'd worn it, the breeze had passed through as if she were wearing angel hair. She'd also pierced her nostril. She'd pushed a carrot up her nose so the hot pin didn't stab through and hit her septum. She concentrated on the TV. God she could use a toke. She wondered if Odette had anything. Darlene didn't know if Odette even smoked dope. She'd never found any or smelled it on her. Darlene was tempted to ask, though knew Odette would probably lie, not from fear, but to be contrary, to make Darlene feel like a degenerate, to be able to thrust that bony little hip of hers and say, See, is it any wonder your marriage is so screwed up? So Darlene hung on, sipping her coffee and staring at the screen. Tomorrow. She'd get buzzed tomorrow with Sylvia. "What's this Benny do that he can't afford a condom?"

"He's assistant manager of a Rent-A-Wreck and— gimme a break will ya, he gave me the watch, didn't he? And his name's Lenny, he's twenty-seven, and what is that thing?"

"A dung beetle."

"It's gross."

175

"It's nature."

Odette shouldered herself forward from the doorway and dropped down beside Darlene on the couch. "Why don't you turn the lights on?"

"Why aren't you on the pill?"

"It's bad for you." Odette lit up another Turkish cigarette. "When's the last time you saw him?"

"I don't know. A week."

Odette sucked her cigarette making it hiss. "Don't you ever do it?"

"Do what?"

Odette wanted to scream. She dragged on her smoke. Twelve bucks a pack. Lenny gave her a fresh one every time he saw her. He'd want to go park on the other side of the cemetery and do it as soon as she was in the car. Odette turned and finally said what she'd been thinking all along. "It's your fault he's down there."

Darlene slapped Odette so hard across the face her palm stung like it'd been scorched. "And what the hell would you—at the grand old age of seven-fucking-teen know?"

They both heard Lenny out front, honking.

"Fuck you!" Odette ran out of the house.

Darlene peeked between the curtains as Odette swung open the car door then threw herself at this Lenny character. Darlene's hand throbbed all the way to the elbow. Then Odette looked up at the window, suspecting her mother of spying. Darlene quickly let the curtains fall closed. Ten-year age difference. Maybe she should get his licence? Who was the guy? She parted the curtain to get another look, but they were gone. And no condom. Darlene thought of that Liberian sailor she once met in the Princeton Hotel beer parlour. Isaac. He was twenty-seven. They'd made it on his peacoat out on the grass of New Brighton Park surrounded by seagull crap, just fifty yards from his ship docked at the Alberta Wheat Pool. He'd smelled like wet burlap. He'd called her a whore afterward. She, too, was seventeen.

Odette had been gone half an hour when the police showed up wanting to talk to Klaus. Now, after having argued with both Klaus and Odette, and after both of them had walked out, Darlene sat alone on the couch and watched the news. The last item was about The Upper Crust. The report didn't say much, and the footage showed only a burned door and a fire truck. She knew the place, of course. Darlene and Klaus used to go for drives all over the city, browsing the bakeries and even making notes on them. They'd both agreed The Upper Crust was ideal, excellent location, good facilities, and an established clientele. He said he'd snap it up in a minute. Well, now it was gone. It seemed a fitting end to the evening. After the news, Darlene watched the shopping channel. She and Sylvia sometimes watched the shopping channel while stoned, Sylvia delivering a caustic commentary on the pathetic cases who actually phoned in and gave out their credit card numbers for blown glass kittens, rings that resembled dead spiders, wigs hand-sewn from children's hair, or the latest video on breast implants. Darlene never confessed to having called in for that breast video herself.

CHAPTER TEN

Moths of the World

K LAUS KNEW WHY Epp's lights were on. Klaus was the one who'd suggested the timer after Epp got robbed one night. Crossing the lawn toward Epp's door, Klaus reflected on the fact that he also knew who robbed Epp—Klaus.

Burning down The Upper Crust wasn't his first desperate act. When Klaus transferred off graveyard, Epp bugged him even more about opening that bakery. Klaus came up with the excuse that it was too expensive. Epp offered his own savings. Klaus, however, maintained it still wasn't enough. More importantly, he said, it was a sure way to ruin their friendship.

"You want that?"

Epp, touched, said no.

"Well then."

"There's gotta be a way."

"Find it, you tell me."

So, a few days later, Epp announced he was going into the marijuana business. They were seated at Epp's kitchen table, and right there in *The Province* was an article on the profits being made by B.C. pot growers producing hydroponic marijuana in their own homes.

Epp quoted, " 'The 1990s will be remembered as the marijuana decade in B.C.' Guys're pullin' in fifty Gs a year!"

"And who are you going to sell it to?"

Epp hadn't thought that far ahead.

"You know anyone who'll buy a pound of pot? You know anyone who'll buy five pounds?"

"Well shit, someone's buyin' it."

"Yeah, the Hell's Angels."

But Epp went ahead and did it anyway, buying lamps and troughs and chemicals and seeds. As the days passed, Klaus watched the seeds sprout and root and turn into little pot plants. Despite his fear of Epp's success, Klaus had to admit he was impressed. He contemplated an anonymous call to the cops. He warned Epp about the penalties.

"There ain't no penalties. I been keepin' a file." And, to Klaus's astonishment, Epp showed him a folder full of newspaper clippings. "And you know what else I been doin'? Goin' down to the courthouse in the mornin' and watchin' the cases. Goddamn guys're waltzin' outa there grinnin'."

Following a pamphlet called *"HIYH: Hemp In Your Home,"* Epp cut the lights back to twelve hours a day after two weeks, to simulate autumn and induce budding. By six weeks, the plants stood a yard tall and were swollen with thick green resin-rich buds that retailed for three thousand dollars a pound. Epp estimated that once the crop was trimmed and dried he'd have about five pounds.

"That's fifteen grand, Klaus! Couple more crops like this we'll be in business!"

"When do you plan to harvest?"

"Book says to give her another ten days."

Five nights later, while Epp was dumping flour at the bakery, Klaus broke in and stole everything, the plants as well as the equipment, and dumped it all in the river, right where, less than a year later, Epp would jump in.

§

Now all Epp's windows were barred and he had that timer. In the window next to the basement door stood Epp's moth collection. Each specimen in a Mexican beer bottle, Carona, because the glass was clear. He found the moths in the bakery, dead below the blue light which lured then zapped them. He took the biggest home each morning and studied them under a Woolworth's magnifying glass. Epp even got himself a book, *Lepidoptera: Butterflies and Moths of the World.* He scotch-taped labels to the bottles, and, tongue probing his cheek as he concentrated, slowly wrote the English and Latin names in his child-like script. Pink underwing—*Catacala concumbens.* Tussock moth—*Notolophus antiqua.* White-lined sphinx—*Celerio lineata.*

Looking through the window, Klaus could see the entire kitchen with its warped arborite counter, dropside toaster, and the remnants of various loaves of raisin bread. An empty birdcage sat on an empty fishtank. Epp's capuchin monkey had scooped the goldfish from the tank and eaten them. The monkey had had the run of the basement suite. Epp liked the way the monkey went through his scalp for nits.

Yet Epp's pets never lasted long. They either died or escaped. He suspected his landlady, Mrs. Beets, of kidnapping and selling the monkey to a Chinese restaurant. A Scottish Catholic, she found the capuchin a satanic burlesque. Epp spent his weekends browsing pet shops, peering into cages at birds and rodents and fish and reptiles. When Epp brought his baby alligator, Leonard, to work, everyone put their finger in its mouth to experience the sawing action of its tiny jaws. When Leonard got loose all the bakers reported sightings: in the toilet, under the sink, in among the barrels of waste dough. Some insisted the thing had grown alarmingly on its diet of mice and yeast. Epp appeared in the afternoons, creeping around trying out the various chirps and trills recommended in the *Crocophiles Handbook* by Roelof van den Schneep. Then one night a loaf of 32-ounce brown sandwich bread was awaiting him, with Leonard's snout protruding from one end and his tail from the other.

Eventually, Epp bought a seventy-five gallon aquarium, stocked it with angel fish, and, on long winter evenings, shut off all lights but the one in the tank, and sat with his chair turned back-to-front resting his chin on his crossed arms, watching the silent cinema of translucent fins drifting like silken lingerie. The fish raised dreamy thoughts of languid ladies, which reinforced Epp's other reason for wanting off graveyard— women.

Every Saturday evening, Epp searched Vancouver's nightclubs for love. With the Vietnamese, Chinese, and Filipino clubs, he fit right in in terms of size. Once, around Christmas, he got drunk enough to get up on the karaoke stage and sing José Feliciano's version of *Feliz Navidad*. But he always ran into a language barrier, and the loud music only made it worse. In the East Indian clubs, the language was no issue, but the women were half his age and twice his size. In other clubs, it was his job or his clothes or his conversation. He avoided the dives down along Hastings Street because, though he drank, Epp did not approve of drugs. Besides, anyone could get a whore, he wanted a wife. As for the more working-class places, the women his age inevitably had too many divorces and too many kids. Sometimes their kids were right there drinking with them.

Epp went through elaborate preparations for his Saturday night quest. First he washed, waxed, and vacuumed his Duster, then he showered, put a new blade in his razor, shaved himself raw, and splashed on Hai Karate. He ironed a shirt on the kitchen table. Finally, he went out, reminding himself to sit up straight so as to appear as tall as possible. The high point in Epp's search was Audrey, who had flying squirrels. He met her at The Blue Boy. Epp hadn't even been trying that night. It was his new chinchilla that did it, a demure, rabbit-like creature with irresistible fur. He carried it inside his jacket as a heater against the January cold. Entranced, Audrey hovered around Epp all evening, stroking the chinchilla and describing her flying squirrels. Epp asked to see them and the date was made. Audrey was Epp's age, the same height, and she also lived in a basement suite. Unlike him, however, she confined her pets to rodents. When he entered her place, the moist rank funk of urine and wet fur smothered him. He looked around and saw cages: hamsters, gerbils, mice, guinea pigs, white rats, all running their wheels, shuffling their shredded newspaper, and eating their young. Epp didn't have to wait long to see the flying squirrels. Audrey had built ledges near the ceiling and the squirrels had nested in the boxes she'd nailed up. They launched themselves at all angles, the fur webbing their legs keeping them airborne as they glided from room to room like flying wash mitts. The suffocating stench was worsened by the fact that Audrey smoked both cigarettes and pot and never opened the windows for fear that the neighbours would smell it and because her squirrels might escape. Still, Epp saw a kindred spirit. He brought her roses that she chopped up and fed to the gerbils. He took her to a vegetarian restaurant because Audrey was adamant about her diet. The last time Epp saw her was the first night he got her into bed and found a nest of baby rats under her pillow.

"Christ, Klaus. I'd stand a better chance of meetin' women if I hung out in a VD clinic." It was Christmas time, and Epp, moved by the spirit of the season, had brewed up a pot of mulled wine. "Take a sniff of this."

Klaus inhaled, but the fumes rocked him back and he held his scorched nose. "What the hell's in there?"

"Take the hairs right outa your snoot, eh." Epp raked around in the pot with a garden claw and came up with a cluster of five-inch nails. "Iron wine. Used to give it to us in the orphanage. Had a tin cup hangin' by a chain. Could just dip yourself up a drink. Good for your blood." Epp ladled up a measure and filled one of the Christmas mugs he'd got with a fill-up at the Petro Can.

Klaus sipped suspiciously and thought of cloves and engine oil.

By eight in the evening they were drunk, and Epp was telling him about the time he ate a trash can full of snow on a bet. An older boy named Diplock had organized the event two days before Christmas 1967. He'd hosed out the can and filled it full of snow from the roof. Epp ate until his teeth ached but kept going because he wanted Diplock to like him. Whenever Epp seemed about to give in, Diplock reminded Epp of the ten percent Diplock was giving him on all the bets.

"That was before Diplock built that bomb. Nabob coffee can and firecrackers. Blew off by accident in the bathroom." Epp became solemn at the memory. "Deaf for three days."

"And Diplock?"

"Looked like someone threw chili at the wall."

Epp had arrived at the orphanage at the age of four with a dislocated shoulder. His mother had jerked his arm so hard to stop his crying she'd popped it from the socket. Then she walked out, leaving him alone in a motel room on the outskirts of Medicine Hat. The cleaning woman found him the following morning.

He'd sat up all night, hugging a pillow and hearing the cars bore by on the Trans Canada. Thirty-five years later, he still couldn't go into motel rooms.

As for his mother, she came to the orphanage when he was thirteen. She was with two men in a Thunderbird and they all went for a drive. It was 1969. The one driving had a big long beard, but wasn't a hippie. He asked Epp what the job prospects were out here, which made Epp feel like an adult. All Epp knew of work, however, was his chore at the orphanage, which was mopping the hall. The other guy was skinny and had sideburns. He asked Epp if he had a line on any pot. His mother, next to Epp in the back, kicked the seat. They went down to the beach where his mother took pictures of him with the freighters in the background. Then she got the one with the beard to take pictures of her and Epp arm in arm. Epp hadn't realized how young she was. They had the same black hair, sharp chin, and short teeth. She chewed gum and had Wrigley's Spearmint breath. When she gripped his arm for the photo, he got an erection. She said she'd mail him copies of the pictures. Dropping him off back at the orphanage, she gave him a twenty-dollar bill. The photographs never came and he never saw her again.

§

When Klaus finally pulled himself away from Epp's back window it was raining again. Walking home, Klaus thought of the city coroner's. The morgue. At that very moment, Epp was lying in one of those deep narrow drawers under a sheet. Monday at ten. Nausea turned the beer in his stomach to a slough. He stopped and leaned forward, hands on his knees. He didn't want to see Epp dead on a slab, he wanted to see him alive, he wanted to see him emerge from a fog of flour at the back of the bakery as if from a sojourn in the desert, grin his goofy grin, and say, "Hi, Klaus."

Passing the cemetery, Klaus saw the black marble gravestones gleaming in the rain. There were white ones that looked like chalk, and over in one corner rows of wooden crosses that reminded him of that poem they'd learned in school about Flanders Field, where the crosses stand row on row. The spicey smell of grass and juniper hedges reminded him of the bitters his father used to drink for indigestion. His dad hated that Flanders Field poem.

Up ahead, an old Valiant with a Rent-A-Wreck bumper sticker and fogged windows, was creaking side-to-side. Klaus crossed the street to avoid it, but a panting female voice reached him through the rain. "Lenny! Lenny! Lenny!" He halted. The Valiant creaked faster. He thought of the frantic panting of milers locked shoulder-to-shoulder in the final lunge for the line. "Lenny!"

Klaus started toward the car, then he turned and walked away. Odette hadn't been much bigger than a bread dough when she was born. A bread dough with raisin eyes and a furious voice. He'd baked her short-bread snowmen at Christmas, heart-shaped cinnamon cookies for Valentines Day, rabbit-shaped chocolate eclairs for Easter, witch's hat cookies for Halloween.

§

After Klaus left Epp's, Stahl crept to the basement door and looked in the window at those bottled moths. Stahl had collected teeth as a kid. He'd mounted them on cards with a dab of Lepages, then labeled them. DOG (incisor), CAT (shearing), RAT (molar), WHALE (molar), HUMAN (cuspid), RATTLESNAKE (fang).

Stahl went home but couldn't sleep. Two double Ballantyne's and he was wide awake. The entire scenario of buying the dope and sticking it in Singh's locker kept looping through his head. Had anyone seen him? And what about fingerprints? He'd forgotten to wipe the lock. Should he go back? But they said the thief always returns to the scene of the crime and that's where he gets nabbed. So in the middle of the night Stahl was pacing. It took hours, but he finally assured himself that by the time Singh tried opening the lock any trace of Stahl's prints would be long gone. As for the original lock, Stahl realized he still had it in his gym bag, which was in his van. He went out and got it and dropped it in the dumpster. Then he climbed into the dumpster and found it. Maybe he should drop it in the dumpster the next block down? He didn't want to be spotted in the alley at night though. He took it inside. For an hour he hunted for a spot in his apartment. He finally decided upon the slot in the wall where he kept his underwear ads.

CHAPTER ELEVEN

The Bargaining Chip

SATURDAY MORNING KLAUS got a call from Keegan.
"Meet me in The Blue Boy."

"About what?"

"About Epp."

Klaus mentioned the police and the morgue.

"All the more reason we talk. Noon?"

Klaus said okay then hung up the phone and looked around the kitchen. Darlene was in the living room pretending not to listen. He thought of last night, the way he'd walked away. He knew that this evening, Saturday, was her night out with Sylvia. Fear burned like a gas flame inside him. How much time did he have before she got fed up? He went down the wooden steps that needed repainting, across the grass that needed cutting,

to the carport that needed sweeping, and headed for the
river to look for Epp. Just to be sure, just in case. He
listened to the news on the way, but there was no more
mention of The Upper Crust. He'd caught the radio
report yesterday and learned the police had no suspects.
The owner, a born-again Christian named Nigel
Spatchcock, claimed everyone loved him and especially
the lord. The police could only surmise a motive of ran-
dom vandalism. They went on to remark that while the
crime rate in the 1990s was actually lower than that of
the 1980s, it had taken on a more erratic nature, which
implied an increasingly psychotic culture.

It was a balmy spring morning. Klaus didn't park in
the bakery lot, but further down where Fraser Street
ended at a barricade of salmonberry bushes thickening
with their new leaves, right where Epp had plunged into
the water. The riverfront was all sawmills, fish packers,
and sawdust piles. Log booms traced the shore like
wooden roads, and the muddy water shone like newly
glazed clay in the sun. That black-beamed barge with its
mountain ridge of sawdust bound for a pulp mill up the
coast lay moored down river. He got out and walked
along the bank.

A shopping cart swelling over with rebar, wrought
iron, and wire, clattered across gravel. Klaus watched
Henry approach. The clatter halted as Henry, wearing
a green garbage bag punched with holes for his arms

and head, splayed his arthritic legs and strained to pick up a cigarette butt. He deposited it in the jam jar in the child seat. Then he proceeded, the soundtrack of his wobble-wheeled cart announcing him well in advance as he travelled his maverick routes along the river.

"Henry."

The clatter ceased and the old tramp peered from the cave holes of his eyes a full minute before recognizing Klaus there on the rocky bank. "Fishenin'?"

"Have you seen Epp?"

"Nothin' but bullheads along here."

"I know. Epp. Have you seen Epp?"

"Cathcart caught a sturgeon." Henry measured out four feet with his palms, then studied the space as if he'd conjured the fish itself. "Nineteen sixty-three."

"Epp. Have you seen Epp?"

The stirred mud of Henry's mind settled. "Epp?"

"Little guy."

Henry seemed unsure, so said what was newest to his memory. "Cops all through here yesterdee." He swung his arm up as if shooing crows and the sunlight rippled wetly over his green plastic. "And dogs. Fished a fella up right down there colour of a turnip."

"You were here?"

He leaned and a worm of saliva dangled then dropped from his mouth. "No sir I was not." He winked cagily then jutted his stubbled chin, meaning he was over

there, on the opposite side of the river, on Mitchell
Island, a hundred yards across the water. Klaus looked.
When he turned back, Henry was laughing soundlessly;
to anyone who didn't know him it looked as if he was
hacking a hairball. He reached inside his collar and
searched his secret slots and pockets and pulled out a set
of jewelled opera glasses on an inlaid ebony stick. He
peered through them, at Klaus, the ground, the rust-
stained warehouse opposite.

When the old man's rattle had receded, Klaus
looked again at the far bank. Sawdust. Mountains of
it. A holding and loading facility with a grain pump to
fill the barges. He watched a toy-like truck climb one
of the slopes, turn, and back slowly out along a flattened ridge, then evacuate its load sandlike down the
grade.

Heading up to The Blue Boy, Klaus couldn't help
recalling the evening a bad actor at another table decided
Klaus had looked at him the wrong way. Klaus had tried
ignoring him, while Epp had watched to see what his
buddy Big Klaus would do.

"Hey! Fat man. I'm talkin' to you." The pig-eyed
thug swaggered over, reached back as if to slam a door,
and cracked Klaus across the ear. "You deaf?"

Skull-scorched with shock, Klaus just sat there.

The other drinkers were watching now, and the man
understood he had an audience and an easy opponent.

His next blow caught Klaus on the cheek.

Klaus sat on, blinking fast and frowning hard.

"I said, you deaf?"

The bouncers arrived before he could get another swing in, and hustled the guy out.

Klaus, meanwhile, just kept staring ahead, as if concentrating, as if trying to recall something important, something he'd forgotten, and needed to know.

"Quarter to, Klaus. We gotta go to work."

Klaus's glass clattered his teeth as he gulped the last of his beer.

The guy was waiting in the parking lot. He got Klaus around the neck. They struggled. Epp circled them, wondering what to do. Then he saw his opening. He stepped to one side and, wearing his steel-toed boots, looped the guy a soccer kick to the balls. He sank like a sack.

"No, he ain't deaf."

§

Klaus entered The Blue Boy and found Keegan sitting with Lou Camponi. Klaus and Camponi shook hands. Curling black hairs poked through Camponi's red polo shirt which stretched taut over the perfect roundness of his stomach.

Keegan pushed a beer across the gold terrycloth.

"How you holdin' up, Klaus?"

"Dandy."

Keegan blew air out his nose. "Yeah, it's all shit for the big bowl." Keegan was in a worse mood than usual. He'd got a collect call last night from Grace down in Reno. She'd run through her thousand-dollar gambling allowance and wanted more. He said like hell. They argued. He said she was drunk, and she said it was his fault Jimmy was in jail. Keegan reminded her Jimmy was the one who broke the cop's jaw, not him; she reminded him who'd taught the boy to box. Then she added another fact, which was that he hadn't visited him, not even once. His own son in jail and he hadn't visited him. Keegan made his usual excuse which was that he'd had union business, his membership needed him. Grace called him a pathetic bastard and said she wanted a divorce. He said good. She started crying. He left the receiver on the arm of the chair and crossed to the sideboard for the Glenfiddich.

When he returned she'd stopped crying and was suggesting he fly down and meet her, a second honeymoon. Grace cozying up and making her voice all husky embarrassed him. Thinking of her cardboard complexion and breath like carpet cleaner, he reminded her that he got motion sickness when he flew. When she said take a bus, he reminded her about his back. That ended the lovey-dovey. She started yelling about their boy being in jail and he's worried about his rear end. He said it wasn't his rear end, it was his tail bone. Then he tried telling her about Epp, but she said don't change the subject. In fact, Keegan hadn't visited Jimmy for the same reason he'd ignored Epp and didn't want anything to do with Stahl: they were losers. They wanted special treatment. What special treatment did he get when he was a kid? Six of them to a bed and diet of potatoes and onions. Finally, Grace said sell her Hummel figurines and send her the money. Keegan told her if she didn't get off the line, they wouldn't have enough to pay for the phone bill let alone her gambling. She accused him of thinking only of money and hung up.

Sitting in The Blue Boy, Keegan asked Klaus if there was any further news.

"No."

Camponi said, "So they've made a positive ID?"

"I'm going down there Monday morning."

"We can only hope," said Keegan.

Klaus wondered what exactly Keegan hoped for, Epp dead or Epp alive.

"We can't do anything about the pay cut, Klaus. They got us three-ways-from-Thursday, so now it's an issue of dignity."

"Dignity?"

"The dignity of our union," said Keegan. "It's a sign of the times. Organized labour's under attack. It's divide and conquer. Back East's already got us chalked off the board. And we can't do dick about it unless we find a bargaining chip."

"What kind of a bargaining chip?" asked Klaus.

Keegan reached inside his jute-coloured coat, came out with his inhalor, looked at it as if he didn't know what it was, put it back, and pulled out his Players and silver lighter. "Something to keep us in the game."

"Epp," said Camponi.

"Leverage," said Keegan.

Klaus watched them. He knew Keegan would probably get bumped out of the union office in the next election. Keegan knew it too. What he was after was something to divert the membership. A victory. A concession. Anything. "You mean blackmail."

Keegan's glance cut toward Camponi.

Camponi leaned in. "No. A bargaining chip. We drop the charges in exchange for a concession."

Klaus endured a moment of panic. "Who's getting charged?"

Keegan looked surprised. "Hell. Bestbuy. Singh, Graves, Wong, the whole lot of the buggers."

"Because they left Epp on graveyard when he had seniority," said Klaus, catching on.

"A locked-in five-year contract," said Keegan. "Guaranteed cost-of-living increase each year."

"What if he's not dead?" said Klaus.

Camponi interlaced his smooth fat fingers over the ball of his belly. "Doesn't really matter."

"Though it would be better, right."

Keegan crushed his unlit cigarette. "Jesus John Christ, Klaus. He's your friend, you'd think you'd want something on his behalf."

Camponi raised a fat conciliatory palm. He had dimpled hands with manicured nails, which made Klaus think of a pasha. "He has sustained trauma," said Camponi. "Very likely injury, massive inconvenience, and humiliation. All at the hands of his employer."

"You're damn right," said Keegan. "I've given my life to this union. Who went to bat for Willie Vickers when he dropped Clyde Graves with a pan? Me. Who got us our birthday's off with pay? Me." Keegan was about to add how he'd passed up visiting his own son in jail for the sake of union business but stopped himself. He fished up a fresh cigarette and lit it. "You think I don't bleed seein' them cut five dollars an hour out of us? I got my son Jimmy doin' two-years-less-a-day because I taught him to stand up for himself. Believe you me if I could do that time in his place I'd be there. But I still maintain the principle that you go down fightin'. You stand up for yourself and your brother. Either that or you're accountable in the next world."

CHAPTER TWELVE

The Meat Draw

AFTER HIS SLEEPLESS NIGHT, Stahl was exhausted Saturday morning when he bought the camera and telephoto lens from Vancouver Pawnbrokers. A near new 105 millimetre lens and body for $900. The clerk put it together and said check it out. Stahl went to the glass door and focussed on a rooming house window across Hastings Street. A sweet and seductive sensation stole through him. He scanned the windows and held on a Native woman wearing nothing but a towel, and brushing her teeth. Stahl turned to the clerk and said okay.

An hour later, at noon, Stahl was chiselling the ice blocking his father's freezer. He visited his father every Saturday and took care of his chores.

"I told you to shut it off and let it melt."

"Why don't you shave? You look like a damn rubby."

The chisel slipped and Stahl gouged himself. He dropped the chisel and gripped his finger, glaring at the black blood oozing from the wound.

"Yer drunk."

Stahl pushed past toward the bathroom.

The old man followed, rubber wheels sucking stickily at the lino. Forty-five years of inhaling flour dust had put him in a wheelchair. An oxygen tank equipped with a mask was strapped to the back so he could take a shot whenever needed. "Noon and you stink of rye." He watched his son struggle bloody-fingered with a bandaid.

"You got bad hands."

"If I got bad hands I got 'em from you."

"Bull-Christly-shit. I got good hands. I always been good with my hands. Played outfield didn't even use a glove."

"Then how come you only got eight fingers?"

"You know damn well how I lost my fingers."

"Yeah, yeah, Red Elton bit 'em off."

"That's right."

"Red Elton must've had sharp teeth."

"Get that bastard! There, right there!"

Stahl pressed a mosquito flat to the wall with his thumb.

"Well don't Jesus just leave it!"

Stahl cleaned away the dead mosquito with toilet paper.

"Buggers're everywhere. I want you to call the fumigator. Got rats too. You stuck me in a place with rats. They're in the walls. I hear 'em."

"Place is only a year old."

"I tell you there's rats. And there's retards. They drool. One guy pissed himself in the card room."

Stahl returned to the kitchen with his father right behind.

"Yer pants are out at the arse."

Stahl reached back and found the hole.

"Don't you wear gonch?"

Stahl considered the iced-up freezer. "No."

"It's not right. Your mother brought you up to wear gonch. A man should wear gonch and be good with his hands."

"Why'd you leave it so long? Why didn't you tell me it was frozen solid?"

"I forgot."

"You open the fridge every day, how could you forget?"

"They fed us Spam for lunch yesterday."

"It's all you ever fed us."

"You seen what we ate in the war you'd be happy to get it."

203

"You ate dog."

"Goddamn right I ate dog. And I'll tell you what else—"

"You ate horse." Stahl resumed chipping the ice.

"I wanna go up to the cemetery later."

"Which one?"

Stahl felt an aggressive silence. "Fraserview. I wanna see your mother."

"She's in Capilano."

His father whacked the wheel of his chair with his cane. "What the bleeding blue blazes you think I don't know where she's buried?"

Stahl pried at the ice on the ceiling of the freezer. "You don't know when your fridge's frozen solid. You don't even know what day it is."

The cane thwacked the formica countertop rattling the dishes in the rack. "Saturday!"

Stahl kept his back to him. "It's Sunday."

"Sunday?"

"Can't you hear the bells?"

"Whataya mean, bells? I don't hear no bells."

"That's because you're deaf too."

"You won't see a red-ass cent."

Stahl squinted in at the freezer, the blanched and frosty air filling his nose. "You haven't got a red-ass cent. I pay your bills, buy your food, everything. Or you forgotten that too?"

"What about my pension?"

"You lost your pension."

"No one can lose a pension."

"You did."

"How?"

Stahl didn't bother answering. "Anyway, it's Capilano. Louise is in Fraserview. Remember Louise? Your daughter?"

His father lashed out with his foot grazing Stahl's calf and sailing his slipper right inside the fridge, where it lodged between a jar of mayonnaise and one of pickled herring. Stahl turned in time to catch the cane descending like an axe handle. He pried it from his father's fist and they stared at each other. Stahl could smell the old man's skin. His skin smelled grey, like unwashed sheets. "Why'd you bury them in separate cemeteries?"

"Gimme my slipper."

"Was it that you didn't want to feel guilty when you visited mom's grave by seeing Louise's, too?"

"My foot's cold."

Louise, Stahl's sister, had killed herself; his mother had died at fifty of lung cancer.

"I told you my foot's cold."

Stahl raised the cane now signaling for silence. He spoke softly, as if it were a wonder. "There. Bells. Only a block away, and you can't hear them."

The old man's eyes dulled as he listened. He appeared lost in a terrible recollection. Then he returned. "'Course I hear 'em."

Stahl retrieved his father's slipper from the fridge. There were no bells. It was Saturday.

§

They stopped at the legion on the way to the cemetery. Stahl held the door and his father rolled down the ramp into the haze of cigarette smoke and war stories. He joined his cronies from the Seaforth Highlanders: the men who'd been there, the men who mattered. They exchanged grunts. Each man sat behind a pack of cigarettes, a glass of beer, and a ticket for the weekly Meat Draw.

Old Stahl lay his ticket down. "Pork?"

"Lamb."

"Lamb? I thought this week was pork." Old Stahl shouted to Cran behind the bar. "Pork?"

"Poultry."

"Poultry?"

This caused grumbling among the veterans.

"They should do a mix," said Young Stahl. "Bit of everything."

His father ignored that and addressed his peers. "I'd rather have pork."

"Poultry's better for you."

"You ever see a poultry plant you won't think so."

"You ever see what pigs eat?"

"I grew up with poultry and pigs and I'll take beef." Old Stahl shouted to Cran. "Chicken or turkey?"

"Chicken."

"I'd rather have turkey."

"Pigs're smarter than dogs," said Young Stahl.

"Don't you tell me about dogs. I know all about dogs. I ate dog in Naples." Old Stahl finished his first beer and drew a second across the terrycloth.

They all knew old Stahl's story of eating dog in Naples.

"See some of these dogs now they eat better than people," said one of the veterans.

"Well we were glad to get it."

"How about mule? Did you eat mule?"

"Get a load of this smart bugger." Old Stahl shook his head at his only begotten son. "Never had to fight for a thing in his life."

Cran came over carrying six mugs of beer in his left hand. His right sleeve was pinned to his shoulder.

"Should have a fish draw," said Young Stahl.

Cran shrugged. "Put it in the Suggestion Box."

"Better for your arteries," said another veteran.

"Don't you tell me about my arteries," said Old Stahl.

They drank in defiant silence, wiped their lipless mouths, then reached for their cigarettes and added to the tobacco haze hanging like smoke over a battlefield.

"Goddamn officers never ate dog," said Old Stahl starting in on his third beer. He held his glass up for all to see. "Look at that. Steady as a plank. You don't see my hand shaking."

Cran rang the triangle announcing the Meat Draw and everyone reached for their tickets. They watched Cran set the fishbowl in the middle of the bar and reach in and stir up the numbers.

"You ready?"

"Shut up and draw!"

Cran pulled out a slip of paper and unfolded it. "Three-one-seven. That's three-seventeen."

A moment of confusion was followed by a shout. "Hey! Hey!" Old Stahl's hand shot up. "Right here. Look. Three-goddamn-one-seven. Ha!" He swung his chair back and rolled across the indoor-outdoor carpet to the bar.

Cran took the ticket to verify the number. His face dropped into a frown. He raised his glasses to see the number better. "This ain't three-seventeen. It's three-eleven."

Old Stahl grabbed the ticket back. "Bull. It's three-seventeen."

"That's a one," said Cran. "See. It's not crossed."

"Since when do you cross a seven?"

Young Stahl endured a spasm of fear and guilt. He had three-one-seven. The vet next to him leaned to see Stahl's ticket and said, "Got the winner right here."

Cringing, young Stahl went up and was awarded a cardboard box full of frozen chicken giblets, while his father glared with the eyes of an enraged rooster. They returned to the table where Old Stahl downed two more beers. To divert him from losing the draw, Young Stahl (commending himself for having shrewdly saved the news), now told him about Epp and the cops. The effect was immediate. Old Stahl returned to life. He shook his head and got angry, but he was delighted. The news reaffirmed his massive disdain for both Keegan and Graves.

"See that. I retire'n the shop goes all to hell. But then that's Keegan for you. I tell you this much, I sure as hell didn't vote for him. No sir. Not me. Unh uh." Now Old Stahl pointed his finger in dire warning. "There's a man who wouldn't piss on you if you were on fire. Out for number one. Don't even visit his kid in jail."

Young Stahl was curious, "How do you know?"

Old Stahl didn't bother looking in his son's direction. "I know." Aloof, Old Stahl drank another beer in silence.

The conversation moved on to the sorry state of

hockey these days. All agreed the players were overpaid and undertalented.

Old Stahl was uninterested. He ordered a double shot of Ballantyne's, downed it, then said, "Let's go."

§

The Fraserview Cemetery commanded a view of the city. Old Stahl put gladiolas on the grave.

"Capilano. You figure that's funny. You're a real piece of work you are." He sat forward in his wheelchair and addressed the gravestone. "Ruth. This little bugger thinks he's a comedian. I knew though, darling, I knew. I could never forget anything about you, sweetie." Stahl watched his father lean to kiss the white marble, and, drunk, topple out of the chair and sprawl across the grave. The old man paddled and squawked until Stahl strolled over and hoisted him back up.

"You pushed me!" Working the wheel with his left hand, the old man drew his cane from its scabbard with his right. He swiped and the stick sang past Stahl's chin. Then he advanced, rolling right over the grave and chopping side-to-side as if clearing jungle. Stahl glanced around and saw, down the hill, that a priest had paused in his eulogy and the mourners had all turned to watch. With the advantage of higher ground his father gained momentum. Stahl jumped aside and the old man plunged past slashing wildly. He ran on down the slope between the monuments toward the interrupted funeral. The mourners, too bewildered by grief to think clearly, realized what was happening too late, and watched the old man in the wheelchair run right up onto the mound of soil waiting graveside.

Later, Stahl went to the Capilano Cemetery by himself, and looked at his sister Louise's grave. For the thousandth time, he envisioned her lying limp among the barnacled rocks, a fourteen-year-old mermaid who'd strayed too close to the shore. Fir and cedar bordered the cemetery and hid the nearby Capilano River in its rush from the North Shore Mountains to Burrard Inlet. The grass was mossy and deep and there was only the river and the wind. Stahl stood very still before the stone because up here he occasionally saw deer. He knew Louise would like that.

§

Stahl lived at Fraser and 50th, straight up the hill from the bakery, on the margins of Vancouver's Little India. Over the years, Stahl had watched the neighbourhood change from Scottish and German in the 1950s and 1960s, to Indian and Chinese in the 1980s and 1990s. He and Sharma, the building's manager, maintained an ongoing feud about who was superior, Europeans or

Indians. Sharma, a Hindu from Fiji, counted his arguments on his fingers: "Chess was invented in India, astronomy was invented in India, medicine was invented in India. You Europeans were living in trees while we had a great civilization."

"Who invented the goddamn airplane you got here on?"

When Stahl finally got home Saturday afternoon, he found Sharma battling a lawnmower, and the alley behind his apartment consumed in dense white smoke. Sharma owned five lawnmowers, all bought secondhand and all useless. On the third floor balcony, meanwhile, his wife and mother and two sisters squatted around a pot shelling peas, their veils shielding them from the fumes.

Stahl swung into his spot and got out with his arm across his face. "You monkey! Who invented the lawnmower, eh?" He ran for the rear entrance while Sharma fiddled and swore and pumped the alley with more smoke.

The first thing Stahl did when he got home was pick up the remote, punch on the TV, and watch the hurtling yellow dot explode on the screen like a paint pellet. It made Stahl think of Clyde Graves. It made him think of those adult war games. Stahl had been surprised to learn Graves was into war games, but Graves had nodded solemnly and said it was true. It was all part of his

Born Again, late-life obsession with health, survival, and the preservation of your natural instincts. Graves had invited him along to have a go. Graves even hinted how great sex was after a day in the bush. Stahl had no desire to imagine Graves in the sack, but he did give the war games a try. As he should've expected, though, they ganged up on him. Middle-aged men in fatigues and face paint surrounded him and blasted away at his crotch, the paint pellets popping and stinging. Stahl figured Graves planned it out, like an initiation. *Get Stahl, get the new guy.* They shot him until Stahl was on the dirt in the foetal position. What was next? Hump him, like Bobby in *Deliverance*? Stahl didn't wait around to find out.

Radio and TV in the background, Stahl sat at the table with a Black Label and three pieces of 99-cents-a-slice ham and pineapple pizza, and studied the head-lines.

OTTAWA STEPS IN TO CAUTION CLARK ON U.S. FISH FIGHT
Canada's foreign affairs minister says the B.C. Premier's threat to cancel a submarine-test treaty could bring unwelcome results.

There it was again. The fucking Americans. Not only fucking up the bakery but stealing fish too.

Said Clark: We're not going to sit back and let the

federal government mismanage our fish stocks the way they have on the east coast.

Which led Stahl to the feds, the equalization payments forked out by taxpaying B.C.ers like him for welfare-rat easterners. We're the ones who should separate. Canada? What Canada? There was no Canada. And as for Quebec, Stahl had never met a Quebecer in his life except those grubby little buggers panhandling downtown. And those Albertans, Jesus, worse than Arabs. Take away the oil they'd be back on the farm.

After supper, Stahl looked over Chapter Six of the textbook for his night school course in business management. DOWNSIZING: The 3 Fs: Be Fast. Be Focused. Be Flexible.

Later he looked at his résumé.

John Howard Stahl

25/12/52

EDUCATION

   Grade Ten: Killarney

EXPERIENCE

   Bestbuy Foods. 28 years. Foreman, 10 years.

RELATED INTERESTS

He tried once again to think of something to put under RELATED INTERESTS. TV? Was that an interest, or just something you did? He had to think about that. He pencilled in the word PROFESSIONAL before EXPE-

RIENCE, looked at it for awhile and decided okay, and left it. Soon he'd add Business Management I to his EDUCATION category. And then he'd give it to Wong. He'd climb those steps to the office and hand it to him personally, all printed up on good paper, with a folder and everything.

The problem of how to approach Wong had occupied Stahl for a year. He needed to establish contact, to make himself known, to develop a rapport. But Wong was aloof. He worked nine-to-five and Stahl did six-to-two. And when Wong did deign to visit the coffee room, he sat at the other table and read the financial pages with such concentration no one dared interrupt. Stahl had searched for Wong's address but found no less than fourteen pages of Wongs in the Greater Vancouver phone book. Once he'd waited in his van and followed Wong home, thereby learning that Wong lived in Shaughnessy, Vancouver's old money neighbourhood of Victorian and Edwardian style mansions. Stahl then returned to the phone book and, after a long search, found the address and corresponding phone number. He memorized them. The information strengthened him, but he had no idea what to do with it.

After leaving Epp's the previous evening, Stahl drove around until midnight listening to the Chat Line on his cell phone. Stahl was addicted to the personal ads. He listened to them every night, often while sitting in his beanbag chair and watching TV. After a year of listening, he'd finally got up the courage five months ago to establish an account so he could respond. His listening took on a new dimension of seriousness. He made notes. He listened carefully, judging their words, their manner, their sincerity. Many, he decided, were hookers. Many others were larks. Those he feared most. What if he gave out his name and number and it was some sort of blackmail or humiliation game? It wasn't safe. So he was cautious. Sometimes he listened to the Gay ads, or to Straight Men Seeking Women, just to pick up tips. He began his selection process by eliminating the women who sounded too confident. He eliminated the achievers, the professionals, the active lifestyle types. He eliminated all university-educated women, and any women taller than him. He lingered over one who was a paraplegic, even though he had an aversion to wheelchairs. He always scrubbed his hands after pushing his father's chair. A woman in a wheelchair would smell like a wheelchair. Still, he imagined this paraplegic woman. According to her ad she was an accountant, she was independent, she loved old movies. He imagined her legs twisted like the limbs of a Calcutta beggar. He imagined her spinal column compressed from too much sitting, and the slow seizing of her intestines, unless, that is, she did exercises. But if someone saw him with a crippled woman they'd think that was all he could get.

He crossed off the paraplegic. What he wanted more than anything, moreso even than sex, was a woman he could take to the annual Bestbuy Christmas party, which, at the time, had been fast approaching. He'd never attended one in all his twenty-eight years at Bestbuy. He wanted to walk in with a woman on his arm. Just to show the bastards. Just to show them. There. See. A woman. Besides, how could he get promoted to supervisor if he never attended the Bestbuy Christmas party? So, after many false starts, he finally recorded a response to an ad. To his shock, she phoned him one Sunday morning while he was masturbating.

His answering machine clicked on. Instead of hanging up the woman began to talk. Naked, Stahl tiptoed to the phone and stared, listening to the female voice as if he'd made contact with an alien species. Anticipating the imminent end of the message space, the woman began speaking faster. "If you are interested in talking, give me a call." She left her number and then added, "Oh, me nyme's 'Elen." Then the click.

Me nyme's 'Elen . . . An accent. Like Mutton's. No, Cockney, like those guys on *On The Buses*. Stahl paced. Oh God. What had he gone and done? He went to the toilet and bent over the bowl as if he might be sick. Helen, her name was Helen. Or was that Ellen? He thought of *Coronation Street*, pub beer, pale skin. He reran the message. "I find this is all a bit dodgy, but

here's for it . . . " Stahl felt like he'd swallowed razor-
wire. It was eleven Sunday morning, but he poured himself a double Ballantyne's to calm down. His day was
ruined. He felt an immediate nostalgia for the safe and
familiar emptiness of all his previous Sundays. When
the rye kicked in, he relaxed a little and went out for a
drive, hit two Canadian Tires, bought new floormats
for his van, then went to a car wash and used the vacu-
um cleaner. Helen. Stahl had never had a girlfriend.

That evening, after an hour of anguished pacing in
front of the telephone, he called her. The first thing she
said was that it was embarrassing, which put Stahl at
ease. He actually laughed a little. They arranged to meet
at seven the following Friday in the Starbucks at
Cambie and 19th. When he hung up, he could hardly
breathe. He went out and walked around the block. A
date. He actually had a date. He obsessed all week,
counting down the days with fear and anticipation. On
Friday, he arrived exactly on time. The place was empty
but for a young Chinese couple and an East Indian
woman. He pulled the newspaper from the wire basket
and sat on the far side, taking deep breaths to relax.
He'd showered then spent over half an hour shaving. As
always before the mirror, he lamented his flat face, beer-
bottle-brown eyes, ashen skin. When he had his shirt
tucked in he turned and looked over his shoulder at
himself. No ass. Narrow shoulders and no ass. His

pants bagged at the rear because there was no bum, only bone. He'd decided against a haircut thinking that would be too obvious. It would pressure the situation. Before leaving, he banged back a double then brushed his teeth. Now he needed to use the bathroom. But what if she arrived and saw him coming out? She'd know he'd been in there. They'd shake hands. If his was damp, she'd be turned off; if his was dry, she'd think he hadn't washed. He stayed where he was and tried concentrating on the paper. Selwyn Romilly had just been elevated to the B.C. Supreme Court bench. Romilly was born in Trinidad. There it was again. Immigrants. And they banded together. They came into the country and hired their own. Look at Wong passing him over and promoting Singh. And it was getting worse. Seven-ten, seven-fifteen . . . He studied the street. Then he looked across the coffee shop and saw that lone East Indian woman smiling inquisitively at him. He watched, rigid with shock, as she gathered her purse and jacket and then joined him at his table.

"I didn't think it was you, either."

Stahl stared as if seated across from a talking cat. She wore black eye liner and gold earrings. For him? For the occasion?

"I mean innit odd how you get an image in your brine about someone's fice."

Stahl nodded.

"What I mean to sye is I can see you're surprised."

Stahl nodded again, then heard himself say, "Coffee?"

"Tye. Earl Grye."

He escaped to the counter feeling both betrayed and intrigued. Weren't *They* supposed to identify themselves? Weren't those the rules? On the wall hung photographs of coffee and tea production, including one of an Indian tea picker, a woman in a sari with a basketful of leaves. Did this Helen have a sari? He glanced her way. Her back was to him. What was that hair style? Bobbed? She wore a gold top, a black necklace, and black jeans. Forty, according to her ad.

When he returned he said, "So, you drink tea."

"Yes. And you drink coffee."

"Yeah."

"Well we've got that strite then 'aven't we."

Stahl found himself stymied for a respone and realized too late that she was being humorous. He tried thinking of something to say. "Do you put the milk in first?"

"I don't tyke milk."

Stahl nodded deeply as though it was probably for the best.

"Were you in church Sunday morning?"

Stahl didn't follow.

"When I called."

Stahl was a Lutheran, though had no idea what that meant. Once, thinking about Graves's latest invitation to church, Stahl had asked Bell if a Lutheran was allowed to go to a Presbyterian church. Bell said it was like switching from Safeway to Super Valu.

"So what exactly do you do at this bykree?"

"I'm the foreman. Of production."

"Production." Helen maintained a look of polite fascination as he described the dough going through the divider, the rounder, the molder, then along the belts that rolled the doughs into logs and dropped them into pans. She, a clerk in the downtown Hudson's Bay store, described how to ring up a sale and do a refund.

"How's your tea?"

"Foyne. How's your coffee?"

"Good, good."

Stahl could see the clock. 7:28. Thirteen minutes since she'd sat down. He was desperate to pee. They hadn't even shaken hands. He crossed his legs and sat forward as if he had a serious question. She sat forward to hear it.

"So you're English."

"That's roight. London."

"How is London?"

"It's doing just foyne."

He laughed too late and too loud and saw her growing uncomfortable.

"I've never been to London."

"Well you'll 'ave to visit sometime then, won't you."

Stahl had never been south of Seattle or east of Calgary. "Are there shoplifters?"

"In London?"

"The store."

Helen described a woman who'd almost made it out the door with an entire set of dishes that morning. "She'd peeled off the magnetic sticker then fit the lot under 'er jumper. You could 'ardly see because she 'ad such enormous breasts. But the store detectives were watching. They're very good, so you best not try anything."

This time Stahl got his laugh off on time. His sister Louise had shoplifted. Perfume. She'd been obsessed by perfume, as if she had an odour she was desperate to disguise. Though clever at getting it out of the stores, the smell always betrayed her, so their mother knew, and the old man beat her. Stahl quoted from his textbook, "'Shoplifting accounts for millions of dollars a year in retail losses.'"

"I really don't care if people steal. I mean personally. Do you?"

Stahl shrugged. "I'm taking a course. Business Management."

"Don't loyke management. I'm shop steward. Managers are bloody bastuds. It's the power that does it to them."

"Where I am the flour goes to their brains," said Stahl, hoping to get a laugh. Helen, however, became serious. "I could never work in a bykree. I'm allergic to wheat. My tongue swells. I very nearly had to have a tracheotomy once."

Stahl had seen a guy on TV who smoked cigarettes through his tracheotomy tube. He began telling her about Donnelly getting his foot run over, and then Epp jumping in the river. "It's graveyard. Causes depression. Bicameral disorder."

But Helen looked dubious. "I once worked nightshift in a hotel. Rather loyked it, actually. Was nice going home when the sun was rising. Didn't feel stuck in the rat race."

With that, a silence spread between them like a sheet of ice. Seven thirty-five. Stahl began to panic. Unable to meet her eyes or think of anything to say, he glanced around the coffee shop and envied the ease of an older couple who didn't need to talk at all.

Helen, too, felt the awkwardness. She discovered her watch. "Crikey. I've got to go." She stood.

Stahl stood.

They stared at each other.

"Where you parked?"

"I took the bus."

He convinced her to accept a ride. When they were in his van Stahl did what he always did, and pressed the button on the side panel locking all the doors. They said you should do that as a precaution, because if a vehicle flipped, unlocked doors tended to pop open, and the roof collapsed. He was about to explain that but Helen didn't seem to have noticed, or wasn't letting on, completely occupied for the moment with securing the shoulderbelt. So she was locked in and Stahl's thoughts veered off down a dark alley. She might shout and punch though, and cause an accident. Or just give in and not struggle at all . . .

"It's not far."

He nodded quick nervous nods.

"I could've walked. Sorry to be such a bother."

If he just kept driving. Convinced her.

"Left here."

He turned right.

Her voice rose. "Left."

"Sorry!" He swung around the block shaking his head at himself. In another few minutes she was pointing out her apartment building and undoing her belt and thanking him so very much. When the door wouldn't open she looked at him. Stahl hurried to unlock it explaining about the roof collapsing, but she was already out and walking away. He put the van in gear and drove slowly down the street watching her in the rearview. She didn't go into that building at all, but crossed two lawns to the third one over. He raised his wrist to his nose and sniffed in search of that something that everyone found so repugnant, and wondered again if that was why Louise had only ever stolen perfume.

When he got home he poured himself a Ballantyne's and turned on the TV. After a moment he got up from his beanbag chair and listened to Helen's message again. Then he erased it. But how to remove it from his memory?

§

Saturday evening Stahl sat in his van watching Bell's apartment, camera and telephoto lens in his lap. Again he raised it to his eye and focused on Bell's window. Wood frame, red curtains, and there, inside, a brick fireplace and mantel with four black panthers on it. They'd had a black panther on their mantel too when he was a kid. Now they were collector's items. If he still had it he'd be able to give it to Bell. Stahl couldn't see Bell. Maybe he wasn't home. Stahl lowered the camera and shut his eyes. Squinting through the lens gave him a headache. Bell occupied the top floor of a gentrified old house in Kitsilano, on Vancouver's West Side. Stahl remembered Kits back in the '60s. He'd drive through staring at all the welfare weasels and their bra-less women. Now, in the 1990s, it was a money neighborhood. Whole shops devoted to chocolate, comic books, vitamins.

He switched the radio on and turned the dial, passing through guitar riffs, car ads, an evangelist shouting "JESUS!" as if he'd whacked his thumb with a hammer. He heard that deejay Danny Finkelman going on about recycling the cubic tons of human hair that barbers in Toronto alone created each year. Closing his eyes, Stahl leaned his forehead on the hard arc of the steering wheel, and wondered again whether the cops would show first thing Monday morning to check Singh's locker, or whether they'd gone right in and already found the bottle and the dope. A tap on the window jerked Stahl upright. Bell. Bell and Mutton.

Bell said, "Are you all right?"

Mutton, meanwhile, smiled his rot-toothed smirk. He'd caught Stahl with his pants down. "Stahly."

Stahl did what he always did when he was scared, he got loud. He took it to them in his foreman's voice. "Hell. You live around here?" He felt his face split like dry birch as he forced a smile.

Bell pointed. "Over there."

"I'm just waiting for my girlfriend." Stahl made a show of leaning to look at the doors of the apartment across the way, then shook his head meaning: Women.

"Girlfriend?" Mutton's disbelief humiliated Stahl. "What's her name, then?"

". . . Louise."

"Louise?"

"Yeah." Stahl tried to think if there was anything wrong with the name Louise. "I better go see what's up." Slipping the camera under his seat, he got out.

Bell was wearing that Tibetan coat with the deodar buttons, and beneath it a low-cut black singlet that revealed his upper chest. "Scott and I are going for a beer. Would you two like to join us?"

Stahl backed up the path toward the apartment. "We got reservations. Supper. At a restaurant."

"After that we're agoin' to The Sweet Surrender," said Mutton, who was decked out in a paisley shirt with wing-tip lapels, a lime green sports coat, white bell-bottoms, and block-heeled shoes that added four inches to his height.

Having backed his way to the apartment intercom, Stahl waved them on their way, then pretended to press one of the numbers and talk to his phantom girlfriend. He watched Mutton and Bell head down the street, noticing how Mutton kept glancing back and shaking his head in disbelief. Finally they turned the corner and were gone. Stahl leaned his forehead on the brick wall above the intercom. Inside the building, the elevator doors parted and a blind woman emerged. She followed the plastic stripping to the door. Her free hand rose to the handle. When she opened it, Stahl whirled. She didn't wear dark glasses, and her sunken eyes looked like burnt raisins. Her face expressed a polite skepticism.

227

She offered her arm. "I'm not too steady. It's a good job they've got that plastic pathway. That carpet's spongy, I don't like a spongy carpet." Her arm waited like a wing in a white sweater. "Just to give me balance."

Stahl reached out, first with both hands, then one, and finally he just held his palm under her elbow, as though offering a robin a perch. As they proceeded along the walkway Stahl checked for Mutton and Bell, but they were gone. In fact they were watching from behind a laurel hedge down at the corner. Yet between the distance, the darkness, and Stahl's body blocking the view, they couldn't see anything.

"Crikey," said Mutton, "the bugger were tellin' the truth."

Bell was vaguely disappointed.

The blind woman said, "Most taxi drivers in Vancouver these days are East Indian. Are you East Indian?"

Stahl stared. "No."

"Your hands are hot."

"Sorry."

"Oh, don't be sorry. Better a hot hand than a cold one. But I suppose Saturday night no one wants to work." She stopped and turned. "Smell those carnations." She held her head high, turning her face slowly side-to-side, basking in the scent of the flowers blooming in the walkway planters. Then she was nodding. "April showers bring May flowers. And May flowers bring June—what?"

Stahl was watching for the cab she must have called. "What? What, what?"

"What do May flowers bring? How does the rest of it go?"

Stahl watched her powdered flannel face, puckered eyelids, the grey gauze of her hair and her pearl earrings set in gold. A little clump of lipstick was stuck in the corner of her mouth, as if she'd eaten red chocolate. A blind old lady dolled up for Saturday night. At that moment Stahl felt sorrow drop over him like a wet tarp. "I don't know. It stops there."

"How can it stop there when the spring is the beginning?" She sounded hurt.

Stahl felt bad, and for a moment tried to think if there were any more lines. He couldn't. "Where do you want to go?"

She frowned as if that should be obvious. "The liquor store."

He opened the door and saw the styrofoam cups, the wrappers, and the beer bottles. He shoveled everything under the seat then helped her in.

Stahl looked around a last time for the cab, then got in behind the wheel.

"Bugs," she said.

"What?"

229

"May flowers bring June bugs."

Stahl started the motor. He didn't think there were any June bugs in Vancouver.

"There are a lot of these van taxis now." She gazed ahead, chin up as if listening. "And June bugs bring July—" She leaned and slapped his thigh. "July skies!"

Stahl put the van in gear and was aware of that slap on his leg all the way to the liquor store. He swung into the lot then turned to her. "What do you want?"

"Well I don't know. I have to browse first."

Stahl tried to understand what was happening here. He watched her release the buckle on her seatbelt and feel for the door handle. He went around and helped her out.

She hugged his arm when they entered the store and whispered up to him, "I love liquor stores. Especially Saturday night." She became wistful. "The bottles clinking, everyone off to a party, everyone dressed to the nines, the perfume, the cologne, the happy chatter. Listen." She made him stop. There was an argument. A cashier refusing to serve an underage kid who insisted he was twenty-eight. She smiled fondly. "The young want to be old, and the old want to be young." Then she said, in a comic German accent, 'Ve are too soon old, and too late shmart.' Port. I think it's a port night. No." She corrected herself. "Southern Comfort. All the flower smells in the air, I want Southern Comfort. A tropical drink, for spring." She gripped his forearm with sudden strength. "August dust. July skies bring August dust." She led him along the aisle using her cane a little jauntily now. "Have you ever been to New Orleans?"

"No."

"Lemons. I'll need lemons. Southern Comfort needs a touch of lemon."

They got the bottle and joined the line.

"And August dust makes September remember, which, in turn, makes October sober." She laughed delightedly, oblivious to the others listening in, free of their opinions due to the simple fact that she didn't see them. She opened her wallet and held it out to the cashier, a cranberry-cheeked boozer whose burst veins mapped dead-end streets on his face. Tears stung Stahl's eyes as he watched her hold her wallet out with such faith in human nature.

When they got back to her apartment, she opened her purse again. "How much do I owe you?"

Looking at her, Stahl thought of her spine, fragile as stacked tea cups. She'd be dead soon. Maybe next winter. The winter often did them in. He wondered what he'd feel when the old man kicked. Relief? No, at that moment Stahl knew it wouldn't be relief, which surprised him. What he'd feel was forlorn, he'd feel forlorn, because not once had the old man ever looked at him in pride. Stahl pressed his palm to his eyes and forced himself to breathe slowly and steadily so she wouldn't suspect he was crying. He hadn't cried since Louise's funeral. He tried working out what the fare would be. "Six bucks."

"Six?" Her eyebrows jumped.

Stahl feared he'd gone too high.

"It's usually twelve. Give yourself a tip. There are loonies in the change pocket."

Stahl made a show of taking money from her purse, but left everything where it was. Then he helped her out. At the elevator she sucked her breath in shock.

"We forgot the lemons!"

"I'll get them."

"There's a grocery around the corner."

"Okay."

He went back along the sidewalk feeling a flicker of enthusiasm, as if they were friends planning an evening of videos. He found the store and entered the damp pantry smell. There was an old cooler, crates of apples, a shelf of tinned soup. He lay three lemons on the glass sheet covering the Scratch & Wins. Three lemons, jackpot. A tall, lean Somali, whose head appeared too small for his body, weighed the fruit.

"How's it goin'?" asked Stahl.

The Somali smiled. "Good."

Stahl smiled back.

At the intercom again, Stahl stared at the names and

numbers. Which was hers? He read the names, looking for one that matched her, an old lady, a blind old lady— an English blind old lady. He eliminated Cho and Jung, Arachuk and Carlucci. Stubble. What kind of name was Stubble? Ashton, Wood, Reed, Pennington. Pennington . . . he repeated it, trying to get an image of what it conjured. Pennington. He pressed the numbers. Each beep goosed his heart rate. No answer. He tried two more. One told him to fuck off or he'd call the cops. Stahl stepped out onto the grass and squinted up at the windows, but he didn't see her, and she, of course, couldn't see him.

CHAPTER THIRTEEN

Sawdust and Bread Crumbs

THE COP ESCORTED KLAUS down to the morgue in a zinc-walled elevator. Then they followed a corridor that sloped away toward an orange door. Movie-like, the door swelled as Klaus approached, spreading in all directions as though he was not walking but falling toward it. He stopped and shut his eyes. It was Monday morning. Seventy-two hours ago, Epp had been alive. Klaus had seen him Friday morning. In one weekend the world had changed. When he opened his eyes he saw the cop watching him.

"Relative?"

"Friend."

The cop nodded as if Klaus had answered correctly.

Klaus reflected how this cop was a sort of Charon, escorting visitors to the dead.

The morgue had a painted grey concrete floor scarred by chemicals. Klaus tried not to breathe the air. The far wall was made up of drawers with metal strap-hinges. It felt like he was in a mausoleum. To his left stood three aluminum dissection troughs, each dangling a hose that fed a lidless toilet. To his right an autopsy was underway behind a plastic curtain. He heard a gush of water and clank of steel tools, then a whoop of laugh-ter. The cop passed a folder to an attendant in a lab coat, who set his coffee down and blew a long puff of air through his moustache as he scanned for the num-bered drawer that corresponded to the number in the file. Klaus's pulse throbbed in his throat. He imagined Epp in one of those drawers, pale and cold. Dead. Epp was dead. The attendant found the number. Klaus heard the click of the handle and watched the drawer slide smoothly out bringing with it a faint scent of insecticide and frost. The attendant was not ceremonious. Tugging at his crotch with one hand, he flipped down the sheet with the other.

"Well?"

Klaus stayed where he was, ten feet away. An oddly impatient frown deformed the corpse's face, as if the sudden light was threatening its sleep. Klaus almost expected it to sit up and start complaining. In death, the head looked Roman, like the bust of an ancient soldier. It had a creased forehead and a large broken nose. For a moment Klaus imagined the man lying dead on the banks of the Danube, the ravens circling while the German tribesmen plundered the corpses. He recalled his dead father. On that occasion, Klaus had been prepared for the face of an irate gargoyle. What he found was placidity, a cosmetic peace utterly at odds with how his father had actually been. It had been the same with his mother. The bags and wrinkles were gone from her eyes. Klaus figured she must have taken them with her to the next world.

"Well?"

Klaus looked up. "No."

"No?"

"It's not him."

"You're sure?"

"It's not him."

When Klaus returned to the land of the living it was ten-twenty A.M. His entire journey to the underworld had lasted twenty minutes.

§

Saturday night, Darlene had knocked on Sylvia's door. When it opened both women burst into tears: Darlene

237

because of Odette, Sylvia because of The Upper Crust. Sylvia, who knew how much opening a shop meant to Darlene, had seen the news. The Upper Crust had been the perfect place.

Darlene described the twentieth anniversary party, culminating with the fight. Darlene had phoned Odette that morning to make up, but there was no answer. She'd called again at one, three, and then at five. Nothing. She finally talked to her machine, suspecting Odette was standing there listening, arms crossed, punishing her.

Sylvia gave Darlene a glass of Chilean red, then sat down at the opposite end of the couch. "She's seventeen."

"I'm forty."

"And at your sexual peak."

"Yeah." Darlene drank down half her glass. "And my husband's a troll."

Sylvia let that hang in the air uncontested.

Darlene picked up on that. She knew Sylvia wanted her to leave Klaus. Darlene told Sylvia about Epp and the cops.

Hearing about that made up for discovering Darlene had excluded her from the anniversary. She knew Darlene was avoiding introducing her to Odette. But Sylvia also knew enough to reserve comment and do the wise thing, which was light up a joint. "Now this stuff is sparkly. Body-high like you're bathing in hot Sprite."

"Klaus'll probably be relieved the place burned down," said Darlene.

"There'll be other bakeries."

"Doesn't matter. He's not going to change."

Sylvia didn't argue.

Darlene took the joint and inhaled. The smoke carried with it all the memories of reefers past; they welcomed her back. She closed her eyes while Sylvia went to the CDs.

"Zakir Hussein?"

Darlene toed off her shoes and curled up her legs. "Sure." The rich tap and toom of the tabla joined them from the speakers. Darlene lay back now with all the ease of an Old Asia Hand and thought of her mud hut in Kathmandu, the Buddha eyes she'd chalked on the wall, her sack of red lentils, her sack of rice, her black hash. A mud house with rice paddies and Himalayan views, and sacred cows ambling the paths. Klaus hadn't fallen in love with the place as she had. He hadn't wanted to travel at all. That was another sign she'd ignored.

Sylvia stretched out on her back on her British India. Her apartment was all cushions and brass and wall hangings. She eyed Darlene there on the couch. "Anyway. To hell with Klaus. What's up with Odette?"

"She hates me."

"She's seventeen."

"I'm tired of that excuse."

239

"How could she hate you? You gave her such a pretty name."

Darlene let the pot buoy her up and became nostalgic. "I liked the sound."

"French."

"Exotic."

"Solid but feminine."

"I also thought of 'Nepal,' but Klaus wouldn't go for it."

"Nepal . . ." Sylvia sounded it out. "Nepal . . ." She nodded. "I like it." She raised her legs up and over her head until her toes touched the floor behind her in a yoga pose. "Maybe Klaus did it."

"Did what?"

"Set that place on fire."

Darlene looked at Sylvia there on the floor in that absurd position. The thought had in fact occurred to her.

Sylvia rolled out of the pose when she saw Darlene's face. "Jesus. I was only kidding."

Darlene poured herself another glass of wine.

"You know what I fear more than anything?" said Sylvia. "Getting old and thinking back on all the things I never tried." She joined Darlene on the couch and began massaging her neck. "You're tight."

"I know."

"When's the last time you got any T.L.C?"

"You sound like Odette."

Sylvia, having finally opened the subject, stuck to it. "When's the last time you had an orgasm?"

Darlene's shoulders seized up.

Sylvia shook her gently. "Have you *ever* had one?"

"One what?"

Sylvia backed off on the subject but massaged harder. They listened to the tabla and sitar.

Darlene said, "I met this Indian woman in Bombay. A widow. She owned the hotel. We talked a lot. She said she'd been married forty-one years and her husband never once saw her naked."

"How long are you going to stand behind that cash register?"

Darlene thought of Pacific Drugs. The fat women buying Sweet Maries by the 50-pack along with a copy of *New Woman* and a jar of hair remover. The coupon clippers backing up the line while the muzak versions of Beatles songs drifted down like nerve gas from hidden speakers. "He'll never quit."

"He won't, but you can. And so can I."

Darlene turned and saw Sylvia's face.

"Why don't you and I open a bakery?"

"You?"

"Us."

"Where?"

"Here. The Upper Crust."

"They burned it down."

Sylvia held both of Darlene's hands. "The damage was nothing. I went and looked."

"When?"

"This afternoon. It needs a new door, some lino, and a good airing out. But that's it. The equipment's fine and so are the shelves. The owner was there and I talked to him. He's ready to bargain. All that arsonist did was lower the price."

§

After the morgue, Klaus drove past The Upper Crust. Other than the plywood nailed across the door and the windows, the place looked untouched. The GOING OUT OF BUSINESS sign was still up, and the shops on either side carried on business as usual. All he'd done is advertise the place. His ineptitude almost made him laugh. He couldn't start a place and he couldn't destroy one.

He ended up in the bakery parking lot, even though Singh had told him to take the day off. He stared at Epp's '74 Duster. The car was the largest single purchase of Epp's life. Four thousand dollars in 1980. Dual carbs, custom hoodlocks, wire-spoke wheels, bucket seats, tuck-and-groove leather interior, a genuine ivory eight ball on top of the stick shift, and blocks on the pedals so he could reach.

While Epp's basement suite stank of old laundry

and animals, his Duster was always pristine, the body washed and waxed and rust free, the seats oiled, the floor vacuumed. He even shampooed the motor. And when he went to a pub he always took up two spots when he parked, so that no one pulled in alongside and scraped his paint.

"What if someone else wants to park?" Klaus once asked.

"Lemme tell you about parkin'. Won't believe what I seen on the TV. Some guy in that Tokyo Japan decides to do this experiment, right. Wants to see how long it takes him to find a parking space downtown 'cause they got this major congestion, see. Guess how long it took. Go on."

Klaus imagined Tokyo traffic. "Three hours."

Epp slapped his thigh in delight. "Four days."

"Days?"

"Four days. Guy drove around four damn days and four damn nights solid before he found a spot. And then guess what happened?"

"What?"

"Didn't have no change for the meter."

At noon Glenda from payroll stepped out and lit a cigarette. When she spotted Klaus she came over.

"I heard."

"Already?"

"Wong called the morgue."

Klaus nodded.

"What are you doing?"

Klaus shrugged.

"Are they going to start looking again?"

"No idea."

Glenda got reflective. She gazed off at the smoke balling from the mill stacks as if reading in it some portent of the afterworld. "I had this dream."

Klaus listened politely. He knew Glenda and Gail. Glenda had once read Klaus's palm at a Bestbuy Christmas party, studying through a magnifying glass the fine lines that curled around the side of his hand. She'd announced that his life-line was long, though in places very thin.

"It was about Epp."

"A dream?"

"He was in a hole."

"Dead?"

"No one dies, Klaus, not really."

Klaus let that pass. "So he didn't drown?"

She drew deeply on her cigarette and shrugged. "A hole. Singing."

"Singing?"

She got defiant at Klaus's tone of disbelief. "I'm just saying what I dreamed."

"Epp couldn't sing."

"He was singing."

244

"Do your dreams come true?"

"I once dreamed my car was all smashed up in an accident?

"What'd you do?"

"Took the bus."

Klaus nodded as if that was the wise thing.

"And that very day I got a call from the cops saying some kid stole my car and wrapped it around a tree."

They were silent awhile. Then she dropped her cigarette, pressed it out with her toe, and went back inside, leaving her smells of powder and perfume and tobacco mingling with that of saw-burnt cedar. When she was gone, Klaus thought of Keegan and Camponi. Three hours they'd talked on Saturday afternoon. The more they'd talked the less recognizable Epp had become. Camponi had pulled a laptop from his briefcase and begun taking everything down, replacing Klaus's words with ones he thought sounded better. Klaus had gone along. It had felt like they were all scrubbing their underwear together against the day the company lawyers demanded they drop their pants in court.

Now Klaus drove the block-and-a-half down to the river, and sat in the car watching the clay-grey water flow past beyond the salmonberry bushes. Salmonberries, always the first fruit of the year. Then came huckleberries. After that it was raspberries and strawberries, then, lastly, blackberries. Directly across the river stood that sawdust yard. The whine of a truck reached him as it swayed slowly up one of the spongy ridges. When the truck was done, it traveled back through the mountain range of mill shavings, appearing and then disappearing.

Klaus looked downriver for the barge Epp had climbed, but it was gone. Then he looked again at those mountains of sawdust on the far side.

Driving up onto the Knight Street Bridge, Klaus then followed the first turn-off and descended into the scrapyards and recycling plants of Mitchell Island. Chainlink fence fringed with spirals of razor wire protected the bottle depots, newsprint recyclers, and automotive yards. Three men in oil-stained overalls and welder's caps sat in bucket seats in front of a shed taking the sun. An old bathtub sprouting a plastic palm tree sat on top of the shed. The men watched him pass with the suspicion of country folk in front of a feed store. Klaus followed the service road, pausing on the far side of the island to watch the expanse of the river's full width and the small freighters ploughing upstream for New Westminster. He continued around until he came to the sawdust yard, Simla Holdings: NO TRESPASSING. He drove on, turned right, and stopped at a guard rail overlooking the river's narrow north arm. It flowed thick and grey with bark and scrapwood. He was directly opposite where he'd parked on the other side. There was the embankment reinforced with concrete slabs, that cottonwood, and those salmonberries. He got out. To his right, sawdust hills climbed forty, fifty, sixty feet up behind a cement block retaining wall. Klaus glanced around and stepped over the guardrail. Gripping the sap-sticky scrub, he crept through the undergrowth until he reached the sawdust. The walls surrounded only three sides, leaving it open to the river. He listened one last time for trucks or voices, then, embarking upon a journey, hiked on into the valley between two high ridges of moist and pungent woodchips.

The terrain climbed steeply and soon he was sweating. He paused and looked around, discovering the view already altered. Below him the river seemed to have grown narrower. He resumed climbing the spongy slope. As he reached the crest a rabble of gulls flapped and cried into the sky and he stood amid a range of dunes. That same feeling of release came over him as when he finally got out of town for a day in forest or farmland, that slackening of the shoulders accompanying a long overdue escape. He sat down, legs straight out, scooped a handful of sawdust and poured it slowly, like bread crumbs, from his palm. He lay back and watched the sky. He hadn't done that in a long time. The disturbed gulls circled and he remembered all the vultures in India. Darlene had wanted to visit the Towers of Silence in Bombay, where the Parsis leave their dead to be picked to bones by vultures. Everywhere they went in India they saw vultures.

Klaus closed his eyes and thought again of Keegan and Camponi. During their session Saturday afternoon in The Blue Boy, they'd questioned Klaus, trying to build a case against the company. Then Camponi said he wanted to see Epp's place. That meant knocking on his landlady's door. Mrs. Beets knew Klaus, and she was full of questions given Epp hadn't been home all weekend. The old woman walked with a cane and wore those black shoes with the block heels, old lady shoes, as Klaus had always referred to them. She wore a headcloth like a charwoman's, and wore a full length fur coat that she'd inherited from her sister.

"Cheaper to put on another layer than raise the heat," she shouted as if reciting a proverb. Her voice was strong and stern, and, due to her deafness, loud.

Klaus, Keegan, Camponi, and Mrs. Beets toured Epp's basement suite.

"He's gone missing you say?"

Klaus nodded.

Mrs. Beets became suspicious. "Or run off." She rapped Keegan on the calf with her cane. "Not a stable man."

Keegan was intrigued. "No?"

Mrs. Beets put her hand to her ear. "What?"

"He wasn't stable?"

"Well I'll not sell it until I find out what's happened to him. It's a good one." She rapped the table leg with her cane.

Camponi opened the fridge and found it empty but for a litre of buttermilk. Then Camponi began going through all the cupboards looking for booze and drugs, but found only cans of Chef Boyardee.

Mrs. Beets clanged the fishtank. "Ate them."

Camponi cupped his hands around his mouth and shouted. "Who? Epp?"

"Looked like Father Michael."

Camponi and Keegan looked to Klaus.

"He had a monkey. A capuchin monkey. It ate the fish in the tank."

They moved on to the bedroom, where Mrs. Beets whacked Epp's blankets raising a cloud of flour. She nodded, as if to say there, look at that.

Camponi wrote on a pad: Was he depressed?

Mrs. Beets read the question. Then she opened the collar of her fur coat and showed them the lump on her neck. "Goiter."

Again Camponi and Keegan looked to Klaus for help, but he shrugged.

They looked at the toilet, which was surprisingly neat. Epp's razor, shaving cream, toothbrush and toothpaste all laid in a row on the back of the sink. In the spare room they found a bale of hay.

"I told him no more dogs'n monkeys. And no goats. I'll not have goats."

When they were back in the kitchen, Mrs. Beets

249

invited them upstairs for beef tea. They declined.

Back at The Blue Boy, Camponi didn't look optimistic.

Keegan said, "Jesus Camponi. What're you on payroll for?"

Camponi turned his hands palms upward. He looked at Klaus. "If Epp shows, keep him hidden."

"Hidden?"

"Stick him in a hotel room."

"Then what?"

"Wait and see how the company's reacting."

Klaus said to Keegan, "Why didn't you act on Epp's letters? He wrote six."

Keegan felt attacked. Klaus was turning on him. Shutting his eyes at the migraine approaching like distant thunder, Keegan thought of the three hundred or so members in their local. He took care of them all. How many problems could he juggle at once? Okay. He dropped one ball. Why did it have to turn out to be a bomb? "If you'd've gone and opened that shop none of this would've happened."

"How do you know how many he wrote?" asked Camponi.

Klaus raised a beer to hide behind. "He told me."

Keegan eyed him, "You led the little bugger on." He glanced at Camponi. "Everyone knew he never meant to open that shop. Was all talk. He don't have the jam."

Then, confronting Klaus, he said, "Epp was the only one dumb enough not to see it. It's your fault he's in the goddamn drink."

Klaus stood, empty beer glass in his fist.

Keegan eyed him as calm as an iguana. "Got a bad conscience, Klaus? Go ahead. That'll make two people you killed."

§

When Klaus sat up, he saw the Knight Street Bridge was already busy with afternoon commuters. The breeze moving across the sawdust carried sap and smoke. He got up wondering what time it was and realized it didn't matter. He'd copped out on Epp, on Darlene, on himself, on Odette. Odette . . . he hadn't talked to her in months.

He walked deeper into the hills. The sawdust dunes extended in every direction. Klaus thought again of the bread crumbs that gathered beneath the slicers: perfect pyramids of crumbs the colour of evening sun on sandstone. In Rajastan, Klaus and Darlene had seen people scrub their pots and pans with sand. That had been in the desert, where the late afternoon sun always turned the dunes pink and vermilion. Once, he and Darlene had wandered out on their own into the desert and made love, the only sound around them the wind. He hadn't hated traveling as much as Darlene thought.

He reached the truck path and stopped. He stood there disappointed by this sign of civilization. Crossing over, he descended the last slope and found himself in the deep crevasse formed between the hillside and the cinderblock wall beyond which sat his car. A path ran along the bottom, a path packed smooth with use. He walked toward the trees and the corrugated gleam of the river. Then he halted and looked back.

"I knew you was here because of them gulls."

Epp's baker's whites looked tie-dyed with dirt. He made no move to approach, but warily stood his ground, as though they were strangers confronting on a path. He carried a length of rebar.

"Epp."

He stepped back. "They still hunting me?"

"No one's hunting you."

"I ain't goin' to no bughouse."

"They were ambulance attendants."

Epp swung the rod in a backhand. "Had dogs all along here Friday."

"You're not in trouble."

"Why didn't you tell 'em? Why didn't you help me?"

Klaus heard the accusation in Epp's voice.

"Goddamn near drowned." Epp tugged up his tramp's pants and Klaus saw he was barefoot.

"Had to kick my boots off."

"Come on. I got my car."

"No the fuck way." Epp backed up again and raised the iron rod to defend himself.

"What're you gonna do, stay out here? What about your place? What about your Duster? What about work?"

Epp spoke as if he'd come to a long meditated decision. "I'm not doing no more graveyard."

"Fine. Tell them."

"Been telling 'em a year!"

Klaus averted his eyes. "When's the last time you ate?"

"Yesterday."

"I'll take you to McDonald's. You like McDonald's."

Epp dug at the packed sawdust with that rod. "Gee, Klaus. I thought we was goin' in on a bakery."

Klaus raised his arms and let them drop.

Then they both turned at the whine of a truck straining uphill.

"They're dumpin' another load."

They stood still and listened to the progress of the truck along its route. When the motor noise faded, Klaus said, "So what are you going to do?"

"Travel."

Epp's certainty surprised Klaus. He actually felt a flicker of jealousy. His first urge was to say, But Epp, you wouldn't know how to travel. "Where?"

Epp spoke with a sullen defiance, as if suspecting Klaus's thoughts. "Up north. Maybe try fishin'. Get out there on the ocean."

"I thought you got seasick."

"No. *You* get seasick." Epp meant their daytrip across to Vancouver Island when Klaus heaved because of a three-foot swell in the Georgia Strait.

Klaus had also heaved on the Dover-to-Ostend ferry.

Epp said, "How'd you know I was here?"

"Because it's where I'd go."

Epp appeared pleased. "I always kind've liked sawdust. Smells good, eh?" Then he got sly. "Check this out." Klaus followed him back along the wall. "Up here." Already at home in the terrain, Epp leaned hard into the hill using the rod like a hiking staff. He stopped at a ledge that Klaus, growing more discerning, could now see was man-made. "This here's my porch." Epp grinned seeing Klaus's confusion. Enjoying himself, Epp reached with the rod and raised a flap of sack as if lifting the hem of a skirt. The burlap sack had been indistinguishable from the sawdust. Klaus leaned and saw a tunnel.

"You're kidding."

"Shit, Klaus. It's great."

Klaus leaned further, peering into the cave.

"Go on."

"I'll wait out here."

"It's easy. Look."

Klaus watched the tunnel suck Epp into itself.

"C'mon!" The sawdust absorbed Epp's voice. Then a light hit Klaus in the eyes and he put up his hand. The light dropped and rolled about the shaft like a blob of mercury. "C'mon."

Klaus glanced around, drew a deep breath, and crawled on into the cool rank tunnel. The dark dropped over him immediately. He paused there on all fours. "Epp?"

Epp's voice was closer than he expected. "Keep coming." The light reappeared to guide him and Klaus soon sat crosslegged in a cave. "Where'd you get that light?"

"Nicked 'er from the ragheads who run the place. Got a whole shitloada stuff the other night."

"They catch you they'll kick your ass so you never sit down again."

"What I did was I opened the gate. Make 'em think it was someone from the outside. An outside job! Get it?" Epp hee-hee'ed.

"Let's have a look." Klaus took the flashlight, a ten-volt dry cell with a lamp like a headlight. "There's no security guard?"

"For sawdust?"

Klaus heard the sarcasm in Epp's tone. Directing the light around, Klaus studied the den. Epp had dragged pallets in to reinforce the walls and ceiling. There were a few pop bottles and a tar bucket and a rearview mirror. "You need a bath."

"I need a beer."

"Smells like a compost heap in here."

"No bugs, though."

"Yeah. And you know why."

"Cedar's poison."

"And you keep inhaling it your brain'll turn to sawdust." Klaus tested the pallet reinforcing the ceiling. Sawdust trickled through. They sat awhile in silence, Klaus idling the beam about and shaking his head. Then he thumbed the light off and they sat in darkness. Klaus heard the bellows-blast of his own breath. "So what have you been doing?"

"Been doin' some thinkin's what I been doin'."

"About what?"

"About you."

Klaus, alarmed at the idea of Epp sitting in this cave thinking about him, tried to sound amused. "Is that right?"

"Uh huh."

"And what's your conclusion?"

"Yer wastin' yer life."

Klaus felt his face burning. "You think so, do you."

"What I can't figure is why."

"And what else do you do in here?"

"You'll laugh."

Klaus was confused. "No I won't."

So, beside him there in the dark, Epp began to sing,

long and loud and right from the stomach, the surrounding sawdust providing perfect acoustics. Klaus listened in an appalled awe.

"*Adeste fidelium*."

"Naw. *Oh Come All Ye Faithful*. I always liked that one. They taught us it in the orphanage." Epp sang it again, and Klaus felt he was sitting with some cedar-crazed anchorite. "Epp."

"I can do *Silent Night* too."

"Epp." Overcome with emotion at Epp's oblivious optimism, Klaus switched on the dry cell and aimed it at him. "Epp!" But Epp was singing, a madman singing to his god. Klaus crawled down the tunnel, swept aside the sack and knelt cringing in the eye-stabbing sunlight. Epp followed.

"You don't like Christmas?"

Klaus gulped at the river breeze. "You know where I was this morning?"

"You're 'posed to've been loadin' the oven."

"The City Coroner." Klaus saw Epp didn't understand. "The morgue. Where they keep the—"

"I know what the morgue is." Epp sat with his knees up and his arms around his shins.

"The police found a body they thought was you."

"Well it ain't."

"I kind of worked that out."

Epp stared at the brick wall directly opposite them.

"How's Donnelly?"

"Donnelly?" Klaus had forgotten all about Donnelly. "I don't know. An operation. He has to have an operation."

"He'll get me."

"Come on. Let's get something to eat."

"He comes from a boxing family. The Donnellys."

"Pizza. How about pizza?" Klaus watched the thought of pizza work in Epp's mind.

"Too many cops in pizza joints."

"Come on."

"Where you parked?" Epp looked around suspiciously, as if coming to the realization that this might all be one elaborate entrapment. He also discovered he'd left his iron rod inside. He slipped in behind the flap of sack.

"Epp." Klaus lifted the sacking but Epp had retreated all the way. "Epp."

"No." The voice came back small but definite as the plunk of a rock into a cave pool.

CHAPTER FOURTEEN

Never a Dull Moment

SINGH HAD BEEN IN BED less than an hour when Ute shook him awake at noon on Monday.

"The police are on the phone."

"What do they want?"

"You."

Singh got up swearing and naked and headed for the phone.

"Your mother's in the kitchen."

Singh came back swearing and naked and pulled on his robe.

His mother stood glaring fearfully at the phone and cracking her knuckles.

"Will you stop that." He picked up the receiver.

The cop described the call regarding Singh's locker and said they'd like to have a look inside.

"Six left, twenty-eight right, fourteen left."

"We'd rather you were present."

"I've had one hour's sleep." Long shifts were one of the obligations of supervisorship. Singh was rarely there less than nine hours at a time, and it was often ten. The shift that just ended had run eleven-and-a-half. The cop didn't care.

Singh dressed and got back into the Volvo, that, still warm, started immediately. The same two cops were waiting with Graves and Wong. McNeil explained that the body in the morgue was not Epp.

Singh, more sarcastic than he intended, said, "What, you think he's in my locker?"

"Like I said, we got a call and want to take a look."

He led them out of the coffee room and into the lockers. He dialed the combination and tugged. When it didn't open he dialed it again. Then he tried it a third time. The cops, Wong, and Graves stood about him in a half-circle.

"Well?"

Singh tried yet again.

"What's the problem, sir?"

Singh yanked at the lock then saw their expressions and what they were thinking. The younger cop's head was filling with TV scenes of butchered body parts wrapped in cellophane; McNeil, older, was considering the more mundane possibilities; Graves's eyes were round and gleaming in hopes of seeing the worst; Wong was amputating Singh from the corporate body.

Singh lifted the lock to examine it. "It's not mine. Look. I had my initials on the back. I had that lock since high school."

McNeil said to his partner, "Go get the bolt cutters."

Ninety minutes later Singh was back in bed. He'd had to explain to Ute about Epp, had asked his mother to please stop cracking her knuckles, taken three Tylenols, and now lay waiting to lose consciousness. When McNeil had unfolded the flap of tinfoil from Singh's locker, neither Graves nor Wong had said a word. The younger cop, gripping the bolt cutters, stepped to the door to secure the escape route. McNeil examined the pale patch of powder then touched his fingertip to it and tasted. He grunted and frowned then grunted again.

"Baby laxative. You got ripped off."

The cops departed. Wong asked Graves to excuse them, which left Singh and Wong alone, with Singh's incriminating locker containing the bottle of rye wide open between them.

"Well, Pat?"

"Have you ever had any complaints about my work?"

"No I haven't."

"Someone planted this stuff."

"That's possible."

"It's the truth."

Wong contemplated the flies in the fluorescent light fixture on the ceiling. Every light fixture in the place was filled with dead flies. "You should clean these things."

Singh looked up. "All right."

Wong didn't know the truth, but did know a position of power, and that right or wrong, Singh was perfectly poised to take the fall. The booze alone was enough. That young Singh didn't know dope from diapers would hardly make any difference to Back East. Of course, Back East would ask how Wong had been such a poor judge of character as to promote him in the first place. Wong looked Singh in the eyes now, letting him know how deeply sad he felt, sad and troubled and disappointed.

"We'll say no more for the moment."

"Someone stuck that stuff in there."

"Get some sleep, Pat."

"Am I fired?"

"No one's fired."

"So you believe me?"

"Let's just let things ride for the present, shall we."

"That leaves me in an uncomfortable position."

Wong leveled a look at Singh. "We're all in an uncomfortable position, Pat. Keegan's threatening to sue."

"Me?"

"Us."

"What if Epp shows?"

"Back East is discussing it now."

§

Two days before, already anticipating the worst, Singh had talked to a lawyer. Dale Snow was an old buddy from U.B.C. Snow had gone on to law school and then into labour relations. Singh had phoned him Saturday afternoon to get things straight, and understand exactly where he stood regarding Epp. After some small talk, Singh had explained the situation, hoping for a simple answer. But Snow was vague. It depends, he'd said. For one thing, he wasn't familiar with the particulars of their contract. Then he'd started outlining variables and going into legalese. Singh had cut him off and asked if he didn't know of any similar cases and what the results had been. Snow knew many cases of workplace injuries, and even death, where the company was found to share legal responsibility, but those usually involved under-maintained machinery. Still, there was more and more coming out on the psychological stress related to shift-work. Incidents of medical leave due to shiftwork were also up. In fact, he had a colleague who'd been approached last year to sit on a committee to help draft an amendment to the Canadian Labour Code regarding shiftwork, but as far as he knew that was all still up in the air.

"So it's not clear?"

"Come on, Pat. I'm a lawyer. The muddier the water the more places to hide."

"Okay. Worst case scenario."

"Worst?"

"Very worst."

"Well, if it ever got to court, and I underline *if*, if it ever got to court, and you were assigned some culpability, any sentence you did get would be suspended—I'm assuming, of course, that you're still the honest and upstanding fellow I knew in fourth year and are not now tarred with a criminal record."

Singh relaxed. "That's the worst?"

"Sort of. The real issue as far as you're concerned is what happens after. From the employer's point of view—no matter what the legal judgment—you're toast. You've cost them nothing but time and money and negative PR."

"They can't fire me?"

"No, but they can lose you. I've seen it happen. And future employers will act like you've got a rape charge next to your name."

"Get out of here."

"You looked at the paper today?"

"Part of it."

"Well you just look at page A8."

Singh found the article. "'Man cleared in sex scandal leaves job?'"

"That's the one."

Singh read the subhead: *Saskatoon jail official claims he had no choice but to accept government's severance offer.* He skimmed the text. The man in question, accused of sexual abuse, had been acquitted on all charges. He was eventually given back-pay but his return to work at the correctional centre was shortlived after the union and prisoners protested. 'I haven't done anything wrong, yet I can't have a job,' said the man.

Singh shouted, "It's not the same thing!"

"Maybe not. But the point is that you were accused. And that's what stays in the mind of the jury."

"There is no jury!"

"Employer then. And if this Opp fellow dies—"

"Epp."

"If this Epp dies, or is seriously injured, that's going on your employment record. Hell, it'll be in the paper."

Singh had had nothing to say after that. He'd hung up and returned to the living room and the TV just in time to hear the theme music for *Hockey Night in Canada*. Ute and his mother were off at the gurdwara, leaving Singh to watch the game. Singh popped the first of his beers and swung his feet up onto the coffee table. The sight of his feet made him think of his skates. He hadn't skated in years. Maybe the next kid would be a boy and they could play hockey. That is, if there was a next one. That is, if he had a job. That is, if he wasn't in jail.

§

Monday morning, after Singh and the cops were gone, Wong climbed the steep steps to his office where Hunt sat waiting. Hunt knew everything. He'd just returned from Seattle. The scars on his face were looking better.

"Never a dull moment around here."

"Keegan's threatening to sue."

Hunt felt a heat in his groin. "The big boys aren't going to like that."

"How do you think I feel?"

"I can tell you how Toronto and New York feel. There's too much union out here."

Wong leaned his head in his hands.

Hunt watched Wong's pain with an almost scientific interest. Yet when a man was down and defeated and Hunt was secure, he was capable of sympathy. "Keegan's desperate. He's out for revenge."

Wong stared at the desktop, thinking that at this

point, military tactics called for a sniper to eliminate Keegan. Or a tribunal and a firing squad. "He wants to take me down with him."

"Well get yourself down to Seattle. New plant. New machinery. Fully automated. Twice the production, half the crew."

"I don't want to go to Seattle."

Hunt sat forward, eyes like nailheads. "Wongo. Wake up. It's Seattle or the shithouse." Hunt shook his head. "You're lucky you're not out on your ass." Then Hunt relented. "So . . ." He clapped his hands and rubbed them enthusiastically. "What time's supper?"

Supper. Wong had forgotten. "Seven."

"I'll bring the wine."

When Wong got home that evening, Mercedes argued in favour of French food, Wong Italian; they settled on Szechuan. Mercedes phoned the caterer while Wong took Enfield and Wesson to McDonald's. The drive gave him more unneeded time for anxiety. He'd been spooning down Maalox and dry-swallowing codeines all weekend. The kids sensed something was up.

Sitting next to Wong in the Jaguar, ten-year-old Enfield said, "Are we moving again?"

Wong kept his eyes on the road. The spring rain rattled the roof like rivets. The wipers were working full speed. "Moving? What makes you think we're moving?"

"I don't know." Then, mind jackrabbiting to a new

topic, he said, "Jason has a cell. It's no good, though. Like it's totally bottom line. The numbers don't glow and it's hardly got no memory."

"It hardly has *any* memory."

"And these Grade Sevens they were like kicking it up and down the hall like it was a puck. Jason was all choked."

"You're not getting a cell phone."

Enfield fiddled with the car radio. "Mr. Jay's a perv."

"The principal?"

"The vice-principal. He's like got really cold hands."

Wong watched his oldest son. "How do you know how cold his hands are?"

"'Cause Enfield's a perv too."

Enfield slugged Wesson and Wesson slugged him back.

"Hey. Enough."

"'Cause like he puts his hand on the back of everyone's neck when you're leaving assembly. He stands at the door counting us."

"He's got a wedding ring," said Wesson.

Enfield spoke with authority: "Lots of married guys're pervs."

§

Wong answered the doorbell and found Hunt holding a

white plastic bag containing two bottles of wine. The wall of rain behind him made it look like he'd stepped directly from a waterfall.

"Wongo. Dunno how you handle this weather."

"Seattle's just as bad."

Hunt ignored the comment and took an interest in the framed photos of Mercedes lining the entranceway. Mercedes in Dr. Sun Yat Sen Memorial Garden, Mercedes in Stanley Park, Mercedes outside the Hotel Vancouver, Mercedes inside the Hotel Vancouver. They went into the den with its oak floor, glassed-in bookshelves, and panelled ceiling. Wong poured them each an ounce of The Balvenie while the grandfather clock tapped like a drip and the rain raged.

Hunt was impressed by the scotch and by the house, which was a Tudor style mansion with six bedrooms. He nodded around. "You seem comfortably set up here."

Wong warily admitted the obvious. "Yes. We'd hoped to stick around."

But Hunt had developed a selective deafness to what he didn't need to hear. They finished their drinks and went into the dining room. Wong introduced Mercedes and immediately disliked the way Hunt held onto her hand. The dinner proceeded at a mass-like pace, the clink of cutlery and occasional cough making the silence that much more awkward. Wong noticed Hunt's glance returning to Mercedes. Whenever another man eyed his wife, Wong saw her again for the first time. She looked good. She'd wisely stayed out of the tropical sun in her youth, and so, at thirty-four, could pass for twenty-four. Her Oriental features and Latin manner were seductive, her hair full and wavy rather than lank and flat. Again Wong noticed Hunt glancing her way. What was Hunt expecting? Was it a part of Bestbuy's code that Wong offer Hunt the Eskimo hospitality of a roll with his wife?

"You like Vancouver?" asked Hunt.

Mercedes didn't hesitate. "Ees dull."

Hunt's eyebrows went up a notch. He was smiling. His gaze cut to Wong then back to Mercedes. "I agree. Dead dull. And dirty." Hunt looked baffled. "Where's all this California lifestyle? We keep hearing about the hot tubs and water skiing, but hell, you go down to that Hastings Street and there's more junkies and losers than Toronto and Montreal combined. Then there's the rain." Hunt shook his head and returned to his food. "On the flight back up from Seattle I read that, technically, Vancouver is a rainforest. Too bad it's not tropical."

Mercedes grew wistful. "You have ever been Honduras?"

"No. Costa Rica. The Caymans. I dove the Cayman Trench." He looked at Wong. "You dive?"

"Caspar he no do anything."

Wong cringed at the sound of his own name, and at

her accent. She was doing it on purpose. Her English was completely fluent, but she always put on the accent when she knew it would bug him. She accused him of being a snob. She said he was a banana: yellow outside, white inside.

Hunt said, "Do you like jazz?"

Mercedes shut her eyes. "I lob jazz." And there at the table she began shimmying her shoulders in her red silk blouse and singing *Girl From Ipanema*. "And salsa. And dancing. I lob dancing."

Hunt was grinning. "Great jazz in Seattle. Great clubs. It's not New York," he admitted, "but compared to here." He shook his head. "Anything is better. *Winnipeg* has more going on than Vancouver. You know from Seattle you can fly to New York for ninety-nine bucks. Domestic flights're half the price down there."

Mercedes contemplated her food. Then she looked at Hunt. "I never been to Nueva York."

"No?"

She pouted. "No."

Wong said, "I don't like the States."

"Caspar afraid he get mugged by negro."

Hunt chuckled. He liked her. Too bad she was wasted on a dud like Wong. "You'll be working under Palmer Mark-Ellis."

"Who?"

"Palmer Mark-Ellis. General manager. Good guy."

271

Hunt saw Wong's face. "Wongo. You can't expect to waltz on down there and scoop the top spot. Start off as supervisor. Be good for you. See the system from the inside."

"Supervisor?"

"Nights."

"*Graveyard* shift supervisor?" Wong was leaning so far over his plate that his tie was in the chili sauce.

Hunt was genuinely perplexed. "Why do they call it graveyard, anyway?"

CHAPTER FIFTEEN

Death of the Dinosaur

A T 5:45 TUESDAY MORNING, Mutton made his usual tour of *The Province*, Vancouver's scandal sheet, which reduced the world to one-word headlines written in blood and flame. *The Province* functioned like a tuning fork, which, along with the intestinal agony of the morning's first cup of industrial-strength coffee, set the deliciously anguished tone of pain and paranoia necessary for each new urban day. Mutton ignored the front page sidebar which stated that the Canucks had been buried by the Colorado Avalanche 4-0 last night, and skimmed until an article hooked him.

BAKER GONE
Bestbuy employee jumps.

A plunge in the river may have been a plunge to the death for a disgruntled Vancouver baker.

An unidentified source stated that Martin Epp, aged 40, suffered a nervous breakdown Friday morning due to job-related stress.

After running over another Bestbuy employee with a forklift, Epp, a longtime Vancouver resident, threw himself into the north arm of the Fraser River. He has not been seen since, despite a full-scale police search.

The source, a Bestbuy employee, stated that Epp's breakdown was due to Bestbuy management's repeated refusal to transfer Epp off graveyard shift despite his twenty-two years seniority.

Union President Hank Keegan reaffirmed the allegation that Epp's requests were ignored.

Said Keegan, "This was typical Bestbuy behaviour. They created an atmosphere of confrontation."

Charges are being laid on Mr. Epp's behalf.

Mutton controlled his glee, removed the page containing the article, stepped from the coffee room, leaned for a look into Singh's office, saw him well occupied, then tiptoed up the steps to the empty office above and switched on the photocopier. He reappeared moments later with twenty copies.

"'Ere ye be laddies, 'ere ye be. Brother Mutton at ye're service. All the news ye need to know. We're goin' ta court. Keegan's grown a backbone. He's plannin' to put Bestbuy in the dock and fry their scabby arses. Can ye no see it? Barbecued Wong on a hook with Graves'n Singh swingin' behind."

"Who's this Bestbuy employee?" said Stahl.

"Well if it were you I'd say it were the first decent thing ye've done in yer life ye poxy wank."

All heads turned to Klaus at the other table. Klaus, however, shrugged in genuine bafflement.

When Singh walked in for the ninth coffee of his shift, everyone watched him. The coffee swayed like black paint in the pyrex pot as he splatted it into his styrofoam cup. When he turned he saw their faces. "What?"

Mutton held up a copy of the article.

When Graves walked in at 7:30 Singh held up the article. When Wong walked in at 9:00 Singh and Graves both held up the article.

Wong batted it aside. "I saw it. We have an informer."

"Keegan," said Graves.

"I just talked to him," said Wong. "He denies it."

"He's lying."

"No. He said he was just about to call the paper himself when he saw it."

"There's nothing illegal in talking to the press."

Wong addressed his attention to Singh for the first time since yesterday's locker business. The law hardly seemed a topic for Mr. Pat Singh to be pronouncing upon.

Graves said, "Klaus Mann. Him and Epp. They were like this." Graves crossed his fingers.

Wong said, "Get him up here."

Two minutes later Klaus was climbing the stairs ahead of Singh, feeling an oddly euphoric relief that it was all coming to a head. Klaus knew he was the obvious suspect. At the top of the stairs he turned to Singh and extended his hand.

"Christ, Klaus. It's not an execution."

"I just want to congratulate you on becoming a father."

"She's not due for seven more weeks."

Klaus smiled the smile of the defeated, wishing that he was indeed going to the noose. "Just in case I forget."

Singh hated emotion. "Let's get this over with so I can go home to bed."

"Think of the dinner conversation this is giving us all."

"I never talk about work at home."

"You should." Klaus felt himself wanting to warn Singh, to tell him to beware, to watch out, but didn't know how, and still didn't know exactly what to beware of. Yourself? Others? Everything? It occured to him to let Singh in on the secret that Epp was holed-up across the river, not five-hundred yards away. Maybe he should tell them all, maybe he should announce that Epp was alive, not exactly well, but living.

In the office, Klaus was not offered a chair. He stood with his hands in his pockets, a small act of insubordination which did not go unnoticed by Wong. Singh and Graves flanked him, and Wong sat at his desk with his mug of pens at one corner and a family photo at the other, while on the blotter in the middle sat the article. Klaus hadn't been up here since Wong interviewed him nearly three years ago for the Supervisorship he'd turned down.

"You've read this?"

"Yes."

"It must have been unpleasant yesterday. The morgue, the corpse, the police."

"At least it wasn't Epp."

Wong sat back gripping his desk. "Of course. That's good news to us all. Do you have a theory?"

"He'll show."

"You think so?" The hopefulness in Wong's voice was almost touching. Then his tone changed. "Did you talk to the paper?"

If only they could fire him, Klaus thought. Force his hand. Make the decision for him. Start him on his way. Then maybe he could open that bakery. Then he'd say yes, if it wasn't too late. Who knows, maybe he could even hire Odette. Why hadn't he thought of that before? But he needed a push and Wong couldn't do anything. Wong knew it and Klaus knew it. So what difference did it make? And besides, would he be taking the fall or the credit? "Wish I had."

Wong sat forward trying to intimidate him, implying this would go down in his file. "Is that right?"

"Yup." And Klaus shoved his hands deeper into his pockets and offered Wong a blunt, defiant stare, meaning go ahead, do your worst.

Wong, however, withdrew. "Well I wish whoever did it had told the other side. Epp was lucky to have a job. You know what the customer reaction's going to be? I'll tell you whose been hurt." Wong pointed. "Those men down there. You think the wage cut was bad? The company's just aching to shut down and go south. Here's one more reason to do it. You're playing into their hands. Thank the squealer for that." Once again Wong levelled his field marshal's glare at Klaus. "Now get out of here. All of you." When they'd left, Wong leaned his head in his hands. Glenda appeared in the doorway.

"Back East on the line."

Wong eyed the beige phone. Then he picked it up. "Wongo!"

Wong had driven Hunt to the airport after supper last night. "Well?"

There was a pause. "Six months."

"Six? I thought we had a year."

"That was before Keegan started talking lawsuit."

"Closed."

278

"Looks like it. I just came out of a meeting. They want to run it as a depot for Seattle bread. Maybe half a dozen guys."

"So there's no way?"

"No."

"No?"

"Well, maybe."

"What?"

"The dollar. If it keeps dropping."

"They're predicting fifty cents U.S.," said Wong, appalled at the enthusiasm rising in his voice.

"But that's not enough."

"What is, blood?"

Hunt hesitated. "Another cut." Wong said nothing so Hunt ploughed ahead. "Bring 'em down to ten bucks even, there's a chance. Between that and the dollar who knows."

"Half pay on a fifty-cent dollar . . . "

"Wongo, what can I tell you?"

"What about Keegan? Does he know?"

"Not until you tell him." Now Hunt's voice took on a tone Wong had never heard before: sincerity. "Look, Caspar, it's numbers. You think we're sitting back here fat and happy, you're wrong. Anyway, it's not us, it's New York."

"Six months."

"Tops," said Hunt.

§

Singh drove home that day thinking of the Canucks last night. Four-zip. That evened the series again at two games each. If it came down to it the house could go. A two-bedroom apartment would do for awhile, three years, maybe even five. His mother and his daughter could share. Singh crossed the Knight Street Bridge and descended into the flatlands of Richmond, passing the polished prefab bunkers labelled SONY, IKEA, FORD in titannic black and red letters. The windows reflected the passing traffic and Singh glimpsed his own car sliding smoothly past like the death dot on a cardiac machine.

Over the following week Klaus visited Epp's den each afternoon but never found him. He'd leave a McDonald's bag just inside the sackcloth door and the next day the food would be gone. Then on Friday a barge appeared under the grain spout to be filled with sawdust. Klaus left the hamburgers and departed along the route he'd worn through the salmonberries on the riverbank. The next day, Saturday, the barge was gone and so was the food. The bag, however, was still there, and on it a note written with a carpenter's pencil in Epp's awkward hand.

Dear Klaus,

Take care of my Duster until I get back will ya. And hey, hope you finally get your act together.
    PS I called the paper

That afternoon when Klaus got home, he opened the basement door and stopped. It was as if the doorway had been bricked over. Instead of the usual basement smells of damp and concrete, he smelled cinnamon. And there was something else: laughter. Darlene's laughter, upstairs. He looked to the ceiling with its exposed joists. He hadn't heard her laughter in months. Maybe even years. In his room he found himself confronted by his cot and the painted sawblades on the wall. He thought of his father sleeping in the back of his bakery. The rooms were nearly identical. Klaus had done his best to avoid turning into him and had turned into him anyway. He dropped to the cot. Laughter again, upstairs. Real laughter, not from the TV. He crept to the foot of the steps and listened.

" . . . and the reason financing is available is that we have a higher rate of success in business than men."

"Small business," Darlene corrected her.

"Our bakery *is* a small business."

"We have to make a business plan," said Darlene.

"I got a guide from the library."

"Will he let us keep the name?"

"He'll charge for it," said Sylvia. "But that's okay. It'll help keep the customers."

"The Upper Crust," said Darlene, listening to the words. "It's good."

Clinging to the railing, Klaus waited until the dizziness stopped. Then he began the longest climb of his life. He went along the hall and into the kitchen. Cookie sheets, muffin pans, bowls, whisks, eggbeater, eggs, flour, raisins, and butter. Sylvia sat sprawled in a chair, knees wide, can of beer on her thigh. One of his beers. Had she been in his room and seen where he kept them? Had they laughed? Would Darlene do that to him? Sylvia raised the beer and an eyebrow in salute, then swallowed a belch.

"Klaus." Darlene had flour on her face. She had flour in her hair too, and white fingerprints on the breasts of her red sweatshirt, as if someone had come up and hugged her from behind.

On the table sat a row of cookies, a row of muffins, and some deformed objects that, he realized with a terrible clarity, were cinnamon buns. Klaus walked across the kitchen feeling like a bug on the floor. He stood before the table a long time considering those deformed cinnamon buns and exactly what they meant. The only surprise was that she hadn't done it sooner.

§

On Saturday, Stahl took his father to the Legion.

"Pork?"

"Pork."

Old Stahl nodded like this time they'd got it right. Then he said to his son, "So you buggers've gone and lost everything we fought for."

Stahl started to argue, but the old man cut him off.

"Don't give me that *It's the Americans* crap."

Yesterday morning Stahl had showed up at work to find not one, but three drivers from Seattle sitting in the coffee room. Mutton and Bell were questioning them, and the drivers admitted that as far as they knew, this was just the beginning, in six months there'd be five trucks a night, every night.

"What about that fella jumped in the river?" asked one of Old Stahl's cronies.

"No one knows."

"Was he drunk?"

Stahl didn't know that either.

"You're foreman," said his father, "what do you know?"

Stahl didn't answer.

"When I was foreman, I knew. I knew when a man was drunk and I knew when a man was sober. That's brotherhood. That's union."

The Meat Draw came and went and Old Stahl lost again. As usual, that signalled the time to leave. Back in the van, he said he wanted to go look at the old Westons, the bakery in which he'd spent so many years. When they got there Old Stahl stared out the window, lips pressed tight, eyes wet with nostalgia for the anonymous brick building awaiting demolition. His voice softened, "See that corner there?"

"There?"

"Right there. That's where the can was. That can's where Red Elton bit my fingers off."

"He must've had sharp teeth."

Old Stahl shook his head as if in awe at a wonder of nature. "Damn right Red had sharp teeth. Don't see teeth like that no more. He was always biting things, beer bottle caps, Brazil nuts."

They sat in silence contemplating the profundity of this fact. Two Wednesdays ago, Stahl had written the final in his Business Management course. Yesterday he'd got his results: A. He considered telling his father, instead he asked something he realized he'd never asked before. "Just why'd he bite your fingers off anyway?"

"You mean I never told you?"

"No."

Old Stahl smiled in pride. "'Cause I took his woman away from him."

284

Young Stahl found that hard to believe. He was about to say *You?* but caught himself. "Yeah?"

The old man nodded deeply. "Your mother."

"Ma?"

"Yup. Come back from our honeymoon and Red bit my wedding ring right off, finger and all." Now Old Stahl shook his head in genuine reflection. "Put the bugger in Riverview."

Stahl gazed straight ahead, considering this.

It began to rain.

Old Stahl squinted out the window. "April showers."

Young Stahl thought of that old blind woman. August dust makes September remember . . . . He shut his eyes to see what it was like being blind. Then he opened them fast. Vulnerable. He felt vulnerable. Like someone could sneak up and get you. How come that old woman hadn't felt that way? He remembered her standing there in the liquor store line-up with her wallet open, all the faith in the world that no one would take advantage of her. Tears burning in his eyes, he looked away so the old man couldn't see him. After a minute he said, "There's a union meeting Thursday. Keegan says it's important. New developments."

"New developments? What happened, Keegan grow a brain?"

Stahl laughed. Then he hesitated. "Wanna come?"

Old Stahl put on a show of indifference, but said,

"Sure. Hell, we'll crank the heat on the bastard and watch him dance."

§

Thursday night Scotty Mutton was the first to arrive at the Cambrian Hall. He carried a plastic bag from the liquor store stamped DRINK RESPONSIBLY. The previous evening the Welsh Men's Choir had held their practise. The hardwood floor was gluey with spilled drinks and blackened with burns from dropped cigarettes. Mutton sat quietly at the back watching his fellow bakers file in grim-faced and subdued. When Bell arrived straight from the gym carrying his wheatgrass juice, Mutton patted the chair next to him. Bell feigned disgust then sat. Dan Donnelly came in on crutches. Everyone crowded around and shook his hand. They'd almost forgotten about him. Now he was back. Stahl arrived pushing his father's wheelchair. Old Stahl raised his hand meaning halt, then surveyed the assembly determining whether or not there was anyone worthy of his proximity. Finding no one, he gave the signal—a cavalry officer's toss of the gloved hand—to proceed to the front. Despite the balmy spring weather, Young Stahl was wearing a toque. Klaus entered, looked about and retreated to a chair in the far corner. Soon the room racketed with the crowd-roar of angry conversation.

Everyone kept a lookout for Keegan. Seven o'clock. Seven-ten. Seven-fifteen. Some of the older bakers went up to shake hands with Old Stahl and agree on how woefully the union had fallen. Young Stahl, meanwhile, tugged the toque down tighter over his head. When Keegan finally appeared, the roar crested then dropped to silence. Keegan was followed by Camponi. They walked to the front where a cloth-covered table awaited.

"There they be lads," announced Mutton, "Mutt'n Jeff."

Keegan expected as much. Steadied by Scotch he sat down, gave Mutton the cold eye, then took a shot from his inhalor. Grace had been over to see Jimmy in the clink, and had come back that afternoon with eyes red from tears, a forty-pounder of vodka, and accusations. As usual, her timing was uncanny. She picked the day he had not just one, but two meetings, first with Wong then this one with the membership. He was just heading out to see Wong at The Blue Boy when Grace had walked in, drunk and defiant, and accused him of abandoning his son. They argued in the hallway. She reminded him she'd been against Jimmy boxing in the first place. He reminded her he never told him to go punch out a cop. She asked why he didn't go see him? He said why bother, he'll be out in two months anyway. At that point Grace sat down on the floor right there in the hall and began to blub. When he stepped past her and headed for the door she stopped sobbing and said, with her smoker's croak, "You don't like people falling down, do you?" That put him in an even worse mood when he met Wong and learned the Vancouver plant was closing in six months. When Wong added that the one remaining chance was another twenty-five percent wage cut contingent upon a fifty-cent Canadian dollar, Keegan had coughed Guiness out his nose. Singh and Graves had been there too. Keegan knew why: the lawsuit. They could already feel the poker up their arses. They were going to get roasted, and wanted to know what was what. Keegan told them they'd learn what was what in court.

Now, at the Cambrian Hall, Keegan cleared his throat. "When I came into the union office in 1985—"

"We were making more than we are now," called Mutton.

"—I inherited a dinosaur."

Mutton reached into his plastic bag and pulled out a lacrosse ball made of dough. He'd stolen five loaves of 24-ounce Ovenjoy White from work and spent an hour at home tearing them up and packing them into balls. He grinned and winked at Bell who, reluctant at first, reached into the bag and took one.

Old Stahl shouted, "Bottom line, Keegan. What's goin' on?"

This won loud agreement.

Once again Keegan cursed Wong's cowardice in

refusing to come to the meeting. "You let me finish I'll tell you exactly what's going on."

Mutton passed the bag along the row and watched the men reach in one after the other and arm themselves.

"You all know Lou Camponi."

Camponi nodded gravely to the membership.

"He's filed a suit against Bestbuy on behalf of Martin Epp. We're takin' 'em to court."

"What's that got to do with our jobs?" shouted Young Stahl. Aware of the men around him, and more importantly of his father next to him, Stahl stood. He saw, from the corners of his eyes, everyone turn to watch him. He reached up and pulled the toque off his head revealing his straw-blond hair. "You wanna sue 'em, fine, sue 'em. But what about us? What about everyone right here?"

Shock at the spectacle of Stahl's hair was overridden by agreement with what he was saying.

"Yeah!"

Keegan saw that just as he'd ignored Epp, he'd ignored Stahl, and now it was costing him. "We're talking the pride of the union, John. We're talking—"

"*Pride*? Where's the pride in being out on the bricks? I worked all my life. I never collected pogey or welfare once and don't intend to now. Just tell us how long we got? Then we can get on with making plans." Stahl's hand went to his hair. He'd got it cut too, fifty-five bucks. He'd never spent fifty-five bucks on a haircut in his life. They'd shampood and dyed it and everything.

Keegan reached for his cigarettes, paused, then pushed them away. He felt the Scotch and the beer going sour in his belly. How had forty-five years in the bakeries come down to this? "Doors'll be shut in six months."

The colour left the face of every man in the room.

Stahl said, "Six?"

"Six."

"Regardless of the wage cut?"

"Regardless of the wage cut."

"And the suit?"

"And regardless of the suit."

Now Stahl held up one of Mutton's bread balls. He reached back to throw—causing Keegan and Camponi to cringe—and hurled it at the floor. It hit like a gunshot. Then he turned and wheeled his father out. Old Stahl waved his cane like a sabre and hooted like they were charging the enemy. Young Stahl's blond head was held high and defiant. His blond crotch tingled. The sound of bread wads slapping the floor all over the hall was followed by footsteps. Mutton, Bell, Donnelly, all of them, joined together in a show of rage. The bread whacked the wood like a volley of bullets entering a board. In minutes the hall was empty. Even Camponi had vanished, leaving Keegan alone up front. When they were gone Keegan managed to light a cigarette despite how badly his hands shook. Three long drags and he'd taken the cigarette down halfway. Then he found his inhalor and clung to it as if it was oxygen. Grace, Jimmy, and now the union. They'd all let him down. He got to his feet, leaned a moment on the table to ride out the dizziness, and moved down the aisle toward the door. Only Klaus had remained in his seat.

"Well?" Keegan's tone seemed to ask whether Klaus was satisfied.

Klaus said nothing. He just stayed where he was amid the flattened balls of flung bread. He thought of Epp and Darlene and Odette. He thought of The Upper Crust. He thought of his old man sleeping on a cot in the back of his bakery with painted sawblades on the wall, the same sawblades that now hung above his own cot.

§

Epp sat at the back of a barge in a hollow he'd scooped from the sawdust. He was eating sunflower seeds and spitting the shells into the glassy wake of seawater fanning out behind. He'd stolen the seeds that morning, plus two gallons of distilled water, a wool seatcover, and a road map of British Columbia from an unlocked truck cab. Then he'd gone aboard the barge, buried himself to the eyes in the fir chips, and waited. Eventually a tug arrived, cut its six-hundred-horse engine and drifted back to lie against the barge like a bull dozing against a wall. The heat from its stack had rippled the air. Epp had stayed still for over an hour while the two men in the wheelroom picked their teeth and drank coffee. Then the engine rumbled up gushing diesel and foam. The tug dropped downstream out of sight. Yet Epp heard the progress of the work, and soon wire hawsers were locked on, the barge released from the dock, and then, imperceptibly at first, the riverbank began receding. He was underway.

Perched high in the sawdust, Epp watched the river curve and kink and then finally open, like two arms flung wide, as the barge reached the sea. To his right lay the Robert's Bank coal port, and to his left stood the cut cliffs edging the University of British Columbia. He was at sea. He was traveling. And he had plans. Maybe he'd check out the Klondike, or Alaska, or try fishing. Or who knows, head east. Then he could hang a right and go south. Mexico. Mexicans were short. He liked that. And he had money in the bank. Dinero. He could give anything a shot.

In the late afternoon, the sun declined toward the west and the barge's stern slipped into shadow. Epp began to feel chilly, so took his seatcover and road map and climbed to the top of the sawdust. In the newly regained warmth of the sun, he looked at the world spread wide around him. The sea gleamed as if scattered with dimes. He shielded his eyes, wondering if there were whales out there. He'd never seen one in the wild. He opened the road map. He knew that if he kept going on up the coast of Canada he'd hit the Queen Charlottes and then Alaska, and that way out west was Japan, where people ate fish raw, and were hunting for parking spots.

Grant Buday is the author of two previous novels, *Under Glass* and *The Venetian*. His collection of short stories, *Monday Night Man*, was a finalist in the 1996 City of Vancouver Book Prize. Two stories from *Monday Night Man* were included in the anthology *Concrete Forest: The New Fiction of Urban Canada* and *The Green Gold Rush*, a screenplay based on the marijuana industry in B.C., was a co-winner of the Praxis Centre for Screenwriters Spring 1998 development workshop. A section from *White Lung* won a Western Magazine Award in 1997.

Mr. Buday is currently at work completing a screenplay based on stories from *Monday Night Man* and a manuscript based upon his travels to India. He lives in Vancouver.